PRAISE FOR KELLIE'S BOOKS

~

"If you're looking for a new author to read, you can't go wrong with Kellie Coates Gilbert."

~**Lisa Wingate**, NY Times bestselling author of *Before We Were Yours*

"Well-drawn, sympathetic characters and graceful language"

~**Library Journal**

"Deft, crisp storytelling"

~**RT Book Reviews**

"Gilbert's heartfelt fiction is always a pleasure to read."

~**Buzzing About Books**

UNDER THE MAUI SKY

THE MAUI ISLAND SERIES BOOK 1

KELLIE COATES GILBERT

UNDER The Maui Sky

Copyright © 2021 by Kellie Coates Gilbert

Published by Amnos Media Group

All rights reserved.

No part of this book may be reproduced in any form or by any electronic or mechanical means, including information storage and retrieval systems, without written permission from the author, except for the use of brief quotations in a book review.

Under The Maui Sky is a work of fiction. Names, characters, places, and incidents are either the product of the author's imagination or are used fictitiously, and any resemblance to actual persons, living or dead, business establishments, events or locales is entirely coincidental.

Cover design: Elizabeth Mackey

This book is dedicated to my author friend, Heather Burch. Your daily critiques made this story so much better. Your friendship blesses me.

ALSO BY KELLIE COATES GILBERT

THE PACIFIC BAY SERIES
Chances Are
Remember Us
Chasing Wind
Between Rains

THE SUN VALLEY SERIES
Sisters
Heartbeats
Changes
Promises

LOVE ON VACATION SERIES
Otherwise Engaged
All Fore Love

TEXAS GOLD SERIES
A Woman of Fortune
Where Rivers Part
A Reason to Stay

What Matters Most

STAND ALONE NOVELS
Mother of Pearl

Available at all retailers

www.kelliecoatesgilbert.com

UNDER A MAUI SKY
MAUI ISLAND SERIES, BOOK 1

Kellie Coates Gilbert

1

Ava Briscoe took a deep breath and leaned into the bamboo-framed mirror above the sink. "Goodness," she thought. "This dress and pearls make me look so...tired." Normally, she wore comfortable, loose-fitted garments, happy and bright-colored. Her half of the closet was filled with tropical prints, linen trousers she loved to roll at the ankle, and flip-flops. Over twenty pairs were lined up on the floor, yet she often slipped into the same favorite pair—soft-sole black Reefs.

She pulled the tube of lipstick to her mouth, then leaned a little closer. As Ava drew the color over her lips, she couldn't help but notice the dark circles under her eyes. No amount of that miracle product she'd ordered online had erased the telltale signs that she hadn't slept in days.

"Mom?" Christel peeked her head through the bathroom door. "I think it's about time."

Ava smiled weakly back at her oldest daughter and pushed the lid back on her lipstick tube. "Okay."

"You alright, Mom?"

Ava forced a brightness in her voice. "Sure, honey. No need

to worry." She moved to join her daughter at the door, smoothed her dress. "I just want to see your dad a minute first."

Christel slowly nodded. "Yeah, okay. Sure. Want me to go with—"

"No," Ava quickly assured her. "I'll join you in a minute."

Christel nodded a second time. "Okay. I love you, Mom."

"I love you, too, baby." Ava turned and took one final glance in the mirror and pressed a stray curl back in place before heading out the door.

Only a few people lingered in the church foyer as she walked across the tiled floor past the open double doors leading outside to the gardens. A slight breeze carried the scent of plumeria and white ginger and blew that stray curl out of place again. Ava gave up and tucked the rogue piece of hair behind her ear for good measure.

Wailea Seaside Chapel was located on Molokini Bluff, with breathtaking ocean views and luxurious grounds. The chapel was like something out of a fairy tale and featured soaring rafters, hand-carved wooden pews, and stained-glass windows. She and Lincoln had been married here, as had her younger daughter, Katie.

A ukulele played from inside the chapel where the others were gathered. She couldn't help herself. The corners of her lips turned up slightly as she recognized her favorite song— "Somewhere Over the Rainbow". The version by Israel Kamakawiwo'ole, or Iz, as people on the island called him.

Her hand reached for the knob on the closed door to the right of the potted Bromeliad plant. She pushed the door ajar slightly, listened to make sure only her husband was in the room. Detecting no one, she entered.

"Lincoln, can you hear that? They're playing our song," she said as she neared her husband. She reached and straightened his tie, then pulled the lapels of that awful suit into alignment.

"Remember? That was the song that was playing that first night at the Grand Wailea."

Ava had been less than twenty years old when she'd met Lincoln Briscoe at her best friend's wedding. She was the maid of honor. Lincoln, the best man.

From the moment she laid eyes on him, her focus was scattered, so filled with nervous anticipation, even giddy. When they were seated next to each other at the luau reception, she couldn't even hold a conversation. Her thoughts danced in infinite directions as they lifted glasses in a toast to their friends, the newly married couple. As their glass clinked, she could picture the scene already—the two of them holding hands on their first date. He would take her for a long, bare-footed walk on Mokapu Beach and watch the sunset behind craggy black rocks and towering palms.

Amazing thing? It had been just like that.

Of course, years of marriage had rubbed the shine off a bit. Raising four children and running a pineapple plantation could do that to a couple. Even so, their marriage had remained solid, reliable. They loved each other. For that, she was grateful.

"Well, honey. I guess it's time." An uninvited tear rolled down Ava's cheek. Fighting to breathe, she leaned and kissed her husband's forehead.

For the last time.

"Thank you, Lincoln," she whispered close to his ear. "You made me very happy. I—Well, I loved you more than I can say." She choked back a sob and straightened. Now was not the time. There would be months, even years, ahead to miss this man— the man she'd shared her life with.

Lincoln was gone. She wasn't sure how she was going to go on without him.

She swept her hand across his chest, gave a final pat.

It was then she noticed a tiny corner from a piece of paper peeking out from the pocket of Lincoln's jacket. Ava scowled with curiosity and tugged the note free, opened it. Scrawled across the paper were the words *Ua ola loko i ke aloha*.

She scowled.

Who in the world had placed the note in her husband's pocket? One of the children, perhaps? And what did the words mean?

After living on Maui for as long as she had, Ava had assimilated into Hawaiian culture to some extent, yet her vocabulary still remained somewhat limited.

"Ava. Sweet *hoaloha*. Are you ready?"

She turned to see her closest friend peeking her head inside the door, her face filled with sympathy. "It's time," her friend said gently.

Ava mustered a weak nod. "Yes, Alani. I'm ready." Ava lifted her chin, bit at her trembling lip. Somehow the words didn't make their way to her heart. She was anything but ready.

She tucked the note inside her bag. With one final look back over her shoulder, she followed her friend out the door.

2

Pali Maui was home to the largest and only remaining pineapple plantation on Maui, boasting acres of pineapples and other tropical fruits. Over the years, Ava and Lincoln had turned the fledgling operation she'd inherited into not only a profitable pineapple enterprise, but also a favorite tourist destination. They'd also raised their four children here. Ava could think of no better place in which to hold a final tribute to her husband, a time for family and friends to gather and share their shock and grief over the loss of a man they loved.

Katie appeared, carrying a plate of what looked to be her luscious kalua pig with a generous helping of pineapple rice on the side. "Mom, you need to eat something," she urged, pressing the plate into Ava's hand.

"Oh, honey. I can't right now." Ava gave her a weak smile. "Maybe later."

Katie hesitated. "Okay, but—"

Ava patted her daughter's arm. "I'm fine, honey. Please don't worry about me."

Funny, she should say that. Of course, they were worrying about her. She was worrying about them.

Ava rubbed her forehead against the ache forming. She couldn't help but wish this day was over and she was free to crawl in bed. She was exhausted and tired of holding a smile on her face.

Glancing back up at her daughter, she caught concern painted on Katie's face and forced brightness into her voice as she reconsidered and reached for the plate. "Look, I can't eat this now, but I'll tell you what—why don't I take the food inside the house and put it in the refrigerator for later." She didn't tell her daughter that doing so would provide an excuse for a quick break from the crowd.

Lincoln knew hundreds of people, and it seemed they were all here now, wanting to express their condolences and share their memories. All his friends were there, his poker club, his golfing buddies and members of the country club. There were bankers and shippers, county officials, and business people from across the island. Moreover, Pali Maui employed hundreds, and nearly all of them were parked on folding lawn chairs with plates of food in hand.

Ava was making her way to the house when she came upon a couple of men talking. She slowed, picking up on their conversation.

"So many times, Lincoln was pushed to go the way of Dole and move the entire enterprise to Costa Rica." Miguel Nakamoa, their operations manager, told the others with an amused laugh. "And you know what Lincoln told them?"

The men leaned in to hear the remaining story, a tale they'd heard often out of Lincoln's own mouth.

"That's right," Mig nodded. "He told them to sit on their pokey pineapple crowns and hush that kind of talk. He would never leave the island."

Ava formed a wry smile as she continued walking, leaving

the men to talk. Actually, it had been her decision to remain on Maui. Her father would have wanted it that way. Lincoln had initially argued, reminding her that becoming a vertically integrated producer was the only way they would prosper and grow. Increasing labor costs on the island would slice away at their profit margin. Land was limited, and distribution options were narrowing. Moving offered remedies to all these issues, and more. "That wouldn't mean we would move, Ava," Lincoln had argued. "We'd simply transfer the planting operation, harvesting, and distribution aspects to Costa Rica."

Pali Maui was located near the town of Wailuku and consisted of nearly eight hundred acres tucked against the western edge of Maui's Kahalawai mountains, near the lush 'Iao Valley. They grew primarily pineapple, but also a few acres of banana, papaya, starfruit, coffee, guava, coconut, mango, and macadamia nuts. Tram buses filled with island visitors toured the grounds twice daily. There was a retail operation that sold fresh items grown on the farm, as well as apparel and souvenirs. Pali Maui was also the home of No Ka 'Oi, a world-famous farm-to-market restaurant with a waiting list nearly two months long. Presenting inventive dishes inspired by the plantation's crops, the beautiful open-air venue was frequently deemed one of the most romantic restaurants on the island.

She'd stood firm against her husband's suggestion to move the operation to Costa Rica. "My dad bought this farm and entrusted it to me, believing we had a responsibility to give back to the people and culture who so graciously extended *e komo mai*. Our family was welcomed with open arms. The island of Maui is our home, Lincoln."

From his expression, she could tell he wanted to say more but refrained. They both knew she'd made up her mind. The matter was closed for further discussion.

Inside the house, Ava found her granddaughter nestled

against the sofa cushions, her attention buried in her phone. She looked up as Ava neared. "Hey, *Tutu*."

The Hawaiian term warmed her heart. "Hey, Willa. What are you doing, sweet girl?"

She shrugged. "Just texting some friends."

Ava extended the plate in her direction. "Would you mind placing this in the refrigerator? I just—well, I need a minute."

Her granddaughter nodded and lifted from the couch. "Sure."

Ava gave Willa a grateful smile and wandered into her bedroom and shut the door, relishing the quiet. She'd barely had a moment to herself since hearing the horrible news. She closed her eyes against the memory of that call, followed by the officers at her door who reported that there had been a fatal accident on what was known as the Road to Hana, a popular winding one-lane road that could turn dangerous in the rain.

Until that moment, she'd had no idea how quickly life could tumble upside down. How her foundation could be pulled from under her feet, leaving her in a free fall.

She wandered across the carpeted floor and folded into a chair next to a bookcase filled with volumes. They both loved to read, Lincoln especially. While she preferred the classics, he was prone to legal thrillers and was an avid John Grisham fan.

He seemed to be everywhere. His voice, his presence. At times, even his smell.

Especially in this room.

Ava kicked off her shoes, leaned against the overstuffed back of the chair, and closed her eyes for a brief rest.

She and Lincoln had married early, barely out of their twenties. It seemed like they had no more vowed their commitment to one another and she became pregnant.

Christel was their oldest. Her daughter was extremely sensitive and known to be a little high-strung, always had been. And very independent. At two, she appeared at their bedroom door wearing a scowl. When asked what was wrong, Christel simply said, "Are you guys going to boss me today?"

The memory brought a smile to Ava's face. It was that same spunk that had propelled her girl onto the dean's list at Loyola. Much to Lincoln's dismay, their daughter had become very liberal, even dying her hair blonde in solidarity with her favorite candidate, Hillary Clinton. Lucky for them, she'd brought her legal talents back home from Chicago and joined the family business. She now managed all the legal and financial aspects of Pali Maui.

Katie was born four years later. Her younger daughter was driven. She refused to grasp the possibility of failure and often took on far too much. Her plate was always overflowing. In addition to raising two girls of her own, she single-handedly expanded Pali Maui to include the tourist aspect of their family business, primarily the retail operation and restaurant. Lucky for them, she married one of the best chefs around. Katie was a brilliant marketer. The family could barely keep up with all her plans.

Then came the boys. Neither were married. Aiden was twenty-five and an EMT. He adored his dad and worked hard to make him proud. Shane was two years younger and attended the University of Hawaii here on the island and had yet to decide his career path. If left up to him, he might never settle down. Lincoln often accused her of coddling their youngest son, but she knew Shane was simply a free spirit who loved his *pau hana*.

She and Lincoln had raised an amazing family—a family that was now her sole responsibility. The burden felt heavy without Lincoln by her side to help shoulder the obligation of influencing, guiding and nurturing them emotionally. Parenting was the one job you never quit, even after your children become adults.

A future without Lincoln seemed a daunting thing. Yet, she

knew this—she had to pick herself up and go on. She had to find a way to survive the loss and keep Pali Maui, its employees, and her family on steady ground.

She would do it, she promised. Ava clenched her fists with determination.

So, help her. She would do it.

3

Katie followed Jon to the car while carrying little Noelle on her hip. Willa walked alongside her gaze glued to her phone.

"Are you sure," Jon asked. "I can hang around until you—"

Katie shook her head and handed Noelle off to him. "No, we need this time together. You go on and get the girls to bed. I'll catch a ride home with Aiden, or maybe Shane." She leaned and gave her husband a peck on the cheek, then watched as he secured Noelle in her car seat.

After clicking his daughter in place, Jon turned to Katie. "There's leftover chicken croissant sandwiches in the cooler if you guys get hungry."

Katie gave him an appreciative smile. Jon believed food healed all hurts and made everything better. "Thanks. I'll let them know."

Her husband moved for the driver's side as Willa climbed in the back seat. "Seat belt, sweetheart," Katie reminded.

"Yeah, I know." Willa rolled her eyes. Her daughter caught the look Jon gave her in the rearview mirror. Ashamed, she stopped with the attitude. "Sorry, Mom. I didn't mean to—"

"It's okay." Katie kissed the ends of her fingers and wiggled them in her daughter's direction, then slowly pressed the door closed. She moved to the driver's door and patted her husband's arm through the open window. "Don't wait up."

Jon nodded, started the engine, and winked at her before slowly pulling forward. She heard him turn on the radio. Music blared from the open window—a tune she recognized as one of his favorites—"Bye, Bye, Bye" by NSYNC—as he made his way down the winding road bordered by plumeria and jacaranda trees in full bloom.

Katie took a deep breath and pulled her arms around herself warding off the slight chill in the breeze blowing in off the spans of turquoise-blue ocean far in the distance. She watched Jon's car until it became but a speck on the horizon, then she turned and slowly walked back in the direction of her mom's house.

Halfway there, she heard her name called.

"Hey, Katie. Over here!"

She squinted in the fading light and discovered her siblings gathered under the gazebo. Strings of tiny white bulbs reflecting in the shadows provided enough light to see a small pile of empty beer bottles on the ground in front of where they sat.

"Do you think that's a good idea?" she asked, pointing.

"Lighten up, sis. We're simply unwinding a bit." Shane reached into the cooler and pulled out another longneck, unscrewed the cap. "In case you hadn't noticed, the past few days have been pretty messed up."

"That's an understatement," Aiden added while staring down at his own bottle.

Christel sat on top of the picnic table. She scooted over and patted the place beside her. "You think we should go check on Mom?" she asked.

Aiden swirled the beer in his bottle. "Nah, give her some space. She hasn't had a minute of time to herself."

They all sat in silence for several seconds before Katie gave in and grabbed a beer from the cooler. "Do you think she's going to be okay?"

Christel nodded. "Oh, sure. What choice does she have? Besides, Mom is a strong lady. It's not like she hasn't had to walk this road before. She lost her mom when she was only a kid, then Grandpa died four years ago."

Katie shook her head. "It's not the same."

"Oh, I know it's not the same as losing your husband," Christel said, relenting. "The point I was trying to make was that Mom is not unacquainted with losing someone she loves. She's the strongest woman I know. I'm sure she'll grieve, but this won't crush her." She glanced between her siblings. "We'll all make sure of that."

Shane placed his elbows on his knees and leaned forward. "I just don't understand what Dad was doing making his way down the Road to Hana in a driving rainstorm. He knows better."

"He *knew* better," Christel corrected. They all paused, shared a moment of collective loss.

"We respond to numerous accidents on that road in good weather," Aiden told them. "The Road to Hana is treacherous during inclement weather. Especially when there's a downpour and an increased risk of rock slides. Tourists might make the mistake of ignoring warnings, but no locals would venture down that winding road in that situation. I agree with Shane." He shook his head. "Doesn't make sense."

Katie glanced over at her oldest brother. Aiden was an EMT here on the island and had seen his share of tragedies, often caused by sheer carelessness. Nothing could have prepared him for the call he received earlier in the week—or the sight of their father's mangled Mercedes at the bottom of that ravine. It'd taken the emergency team nearly an hour to maneuver the steep incline covered with thick foliage to retrieve their dad's body from the wreckage. She suspected Aiden had gotten very little sleep since. No doubt, each time he closed his eyes he saw it all again.

Her throat grew thick at the thought.

She forced a brightness into her voice she didn't feel inside and tried to change the subject. "Well, it was a great service."

Christel nodded with enthusiasm. "Yeah, it really was. Elta's message was very comforting. And I'm glad Alani was there to lend support."

Katie took a deep breath. "Yeah, Mom's really going to need her in the coming days. I mean, you know she's going to hide her feelings from all of us. Maybe Alani can be that safe place for her to—"

"Who are you kidding?" Christel argued. "Mom isn't the sort to wallow. My guess is she won't share what she's feeling with anyone. Maybe not even herself."

Shane rolled his eyes. "Oh, here we go. You're not a shrink, Christel. You can't get inside Mom's head and know what she thinks and feels."

Christel scowled and threw her bottle cap at him. "I recognize I'm not a shrink, idiot. And I use that term only in the most loving manner. But I know our mom." She pointed her finger in his direction. "Mark my words. She won't open up about any of this to anyone—not even Alani."

Katie tended to agree with her sister. While her mother may not openly share her feelings, she definitely had them.

The night of the accident, her mother had called them all and told them to come to the house immediately. She refrained from sharing the grim news until they were all together. Katie was the first to arrive. While her mother's face was stoic, her expression couldn't hide that there was clearly something terribly wrong. Yet it was Aiden's face that told the story. He had been the one to show up with the police and break the news to their mother. An assignment no child, even if grown, should ever have to shoulder.

She couldn't remember who had been the one to call Alani, her mother's longest and dearest friend. Her husband, Elta, was the pastor at Wailea Seaside Chapel, the church where they'd held her father's service today. After learning the horrible news, Alani and Elta rushed to the house and did what they could to provide spiritual support. Alani was known to be outspoken when it came to her faith, and she didn't remain quiet about it that day. She grabbed her friend's shoulders, looked her in the eyes and said, "Ava, you listen to me. Death is not the end. You know that, right?" Using dimpled fingers, she pushed a strand of damp hair off Ava's forehead. "God has a plan, and he won't leave you alone in this."

Katie's mom had simply given her a blank look, unable to absorb any comfort. She'd lost the man she'd been married to for over thirty years without even a chance to say goodbye.

Christel jumped up and waved her arm toward the house. "C'mon, Katie. Let's go check on Mom. Then let's get the sleeping bags. I propose we have a sleepover."

"Out here?" Shane asked.

"Yup. Just like when we were kids," Christel quickly answered. From her expression, her mind was made up. She had a plan and was reluctant to take no for an answer.

Katie hesitated. "I'd have to text Jon and let him know not to expect me home tonight."

Aiden stood, wiped at his eyes. Clearly, he was struggling. Perhaps the alcohol had dug up emotions he wanted to remain buried. Either way, he lifted his chin and announced, "Count me in."

Christel clapped her hands. "Great. Let's go," she told Katie, savoring the fact she'd talked her siblings into an all-nighter.

Katie nodded and followed her inside. On the way, she texted Jon.

They found their mother in her room. She sat in an armchair next to the bookcase, sound asleep with one of their father's shirts held tightly against her. Katie grabbed the coverlet from the bottom of her parents' king-size bed and laid it over her mother. "Poor thing," she whispered. "She was, no doubt, exhausted."

After making sure their mom was properly covered, they turned off the light and headed down the familiar hallway lined with framed photos of their family. There were shots of the girls in brightly colored matching dresses with floral leis around their necks. There was an image of Aiden surfing a rare break in Peahi. The photo that always made her laugh no matter how many times she stopped in the hall to gaze at it was the one of Shane when he was twelve. He sat on a ceramic toilet mounted inside a bathtub on wheels. With the help of their father, he'd motorized the tub. For weeks, he drove that silly thing around Pali Maui until her little brother crashed it into the side of the packing building, nearly taking out the conveyor that carried freshly picked pineapples to be waxed.

At the end of the hall was a shot of her parents taken at one of Alani's *Te Au Kané* luaus. In the photo's background, her son, Ori, and a buddy of his carried a whole roasted pig taken fresh out of the underground emu. No one put on a better luau than Alani Kané, not even the resort hotels along Ka'anipali. Her parents looked so happy in that pic.

"Are you coming?" Christel asked impatiently. She waved her sister on, urging her to hurry up.

Katie swallowed emotion and followed her sister to the bedroom at the rear of the house, the one that had been Christel's. Pictures of Hilary Clinton and Ruth Bader Ginsberg still remained on the wall.

Together, they dug in the closet and retrieved the sleeping

bags. Then they pulled pillows from the bed and lumbered out with loaded arms to meet back up with the boys.

"What took you so long?" Shane demanded. "We thought you'd changed your minds and slipped into comfortable beds, leaving us out here to fend for ourselves."

"Complain, and you can get the bags yourself next time," Katie quipped, sounding a lot like she had back in junior high when her brothers didn't seem to think she did anything right or fast enough. She tossed her armload of bedding at Shane, nearly knocking him off his feet.

She'd always thought her brothers were both a bit spoiled. She'd told her mom that many times and had complained it wasn't fair. Always, her mother answered, "Life isn't always fair, Katie girl. But it's unfair to everyone. In that, I guess we can count on life being fair, after all."

The saying had always confused her. So much so that she hadn't bothered to argue. There was no need, really. The fact remained that her brothers were spoiled. That was that. No one, and no convoluted quote, could change her mind on that point.

Christel passed out pillows while the two boys positioned the sleeping bags on the grass-covered space just outside the gazebo.

"Shoot, we need something underneath, don't you think?" Katie asked. "The ground can get cold in the early morning hours."

Shane brushed her off with a wave. "Eh, we don't need anything. We live in Maui. How cold can it get, for goodness sake? Besides, where's your sense of adventure?"

Katie parked her hands on her hips. "I'm adventurous. I'm also a realist. We're going to get cold." Despite her well-argued point, she shrugged and unzipped her bag. She climbed in, clothes and all. "Well, what are you waiting for?" she asked the rest of them.

Minutes later, they were all zipped up into their bags. Together, they laid on their backs, gazing at the star-filled sky just like they had as children. The air was warm and filled with the scent of plumeria and pineapple.

In a similar instance, all would seem well with the world. But tonight, they were no longer children, safe and secure. They were adults who had suffered a loss. The four of them were here, together, trying to heal gaping holes in their hearts.

Their father was gone.

In many ways, nothing would ever be completely right again.

4

The weeks following the funeral had seemed the longest in Christel's thirty-four years on earth, surpassing even her divorce two years ago. Grief had been sharp as a knife, often stabbing her heart at the most unexpected times. For example, she'd been in Costco, filling her cart with groceries for both her and her mother, when she reached for a bag of frozen hot chicken wings, her dad's favorite. Her eyes had immediately filled with tears.

Her mind drifted back to Sunday afternoons spent on the sofa in the den watching football with her father. He could consume unbelievable quantities of wings. "Panda Bear, be a sweetie and grab me some more ranch," he'd say, holding up the empty dip bowl.

"Dad, not now. We're down to the two-minute warning!"

With tears streaming, Christel reached for the freezer handle and pulled the door open, placed the bag back inside. She struggled to breathe as she listened to the door slam shut, then pushed the cart on down the aisle.

Early after the accident, Christel and her siblings had an extended family meeting. None of them wanted their mother left alone, at least for a while. One of them would have to move in and stay with her.

Katie quickly argued she couldn't step up and do it. She had a family at home to consider. Aiden's schedule was erratic and often pulled him away for extended periods. Shane was, well... not always dependable. That left her, the oldest. The responsible one. The one who always stepped in and made sure everything was taken care of. The fixer, the one who put her needs aside for the better good. The one who might be a little resentful of her role in the family.

Placing her own feelings aside, Christel agreed to move in with her mom temporarily, leaving her own place in Pa'ia vacant. While she loved her house in the little residential enclave known as Maui by the Sea, buying the property had stretched her financially. She was counting on the long-term investment aspect of the purchase outweighing the risk.

Agreeing to stay on with her mother for a couple of weeks wasn't entirely a huge sacrifice. Truth was, she spent most of her time at Pali Maui anyway.

Besides, her mother needed her. The time together was good for both of them.

Apparently, it didn't matter if you were a grown-up. This kind of tragedy turned you into a five-year-old again. You found yourself reaching for your mom, even if mentally, desperately wanting everything to be okay.

And it was, for the most part—okay. Her mother was the strongest woman she'd ever known. Despite her soft, gentle nature, she was surprisingly resilient. She demanded the same from the people she loved.

Yet, that resilience had a slight crack in it.

In the middle of the night, Christel had awakened when she heard a noise coming from downstairs. After slipping on her robe, she tiptoed down the stairs carrying her high school baton high over her head, which was stupid really—Pali Maui had more than sufficient security systems in place. That included the main house.

Anyway, as she neared the bottom step, she heard her mom humming.

"Mom?" she said, letting the baton fall to her side. "What in the world are you doing? It's two o'clock in the morning."

Her mother looked up at her, smiling. "I was hungry and thought I'd scramble myself a quick egg. Then I remembered I had one of Alani's handwritten recipes tucked away, the one for her Loco Moco dish with the secret ingredients." She gave Christel a wink, then turned and reached across the counter for a spatula. "I couldn't get that silly dish off my mind."

Her mother used the spatula to turn some ground beef in the pan on the stove. "My, I haven't had a craving like that since, well...not since I was pregnant with you. Back then, all I wanted was lima beans and peanut butter. Not together, of course. But I couldn't get enough of either one."

Christel looked at her as if she was crazy. "Mom? It's two o'clock in the morning," she repeated, fighting the need to yawn.

Her mother waved her off. "Sleep is overrated." The look she threw her way was filled with impatience. "And I told you, I was hungry."

Christel relented and moved to where her mom stood in bare feet. "Here, let me do that for you."

Her mother didn't argue. She handed over the spatula before moving to the other side of the kitchen island, where she sank onto a bar stool. She swiveled to face the open retractable doors. While still dark outside, just beyond the lanai was a marvelous view of sprawling pineapple fields and the ocean in the distance. "Don't forget Alani's secret additions," her mom reminded. "She puts coconut and pineapple juice in the rice."

Christel raised her brow. "She does?"

Her mother turned to face her. "I told you that a long time

ago." Her mom paused as if reconsidering. "Or, maybe that was Katie." She let out an embarrassed laugh. "I'm losing my mind. Anyway, the recipe is on the counter. Follow it."

Christel and her mom loaded their plates with rice topped with beef patties and fried eggs smothered in gravy, enjoying every delicious bite while gazing at the stars in silence. Suddenly, her mother broke the quiet with gut-filled laughter. "Who in the world named this thing Loco Moco?"

Christel shrugged and took another bite. "Who cares? This is crazy good."

It was then that she looked over and noticed the tear sliding down her mother's cheek. "Your father...he loved this dish."

Christel let her fork drop to the plate. She swallowed. Sometimes all a person needed was for someone to listen. "What do you miss most?" she asked.

Her mother looked up at her. "Everything," she whispered.

CHRISTEL SLOWED her recently purchased Mazda Miata and turned onto the long lane leading to Pali Maui. Her dad had helped her pick out the car just last month after her decision to trade in her dependable Volkswagon. "Live a little," he'd urged when she'd balked at his recommended purchase. "It's energy-efficient, just like you want, but it also screams adventure. This car was made for you, Panda Bear."

As if in his memory, she gunned the engine and savored the way the motor roared to life. Minutes later, she pulled in front of the building that housed the business offices. She should walk over and check on her mom but thought better of it. She was short on time.

She'd just returned from her house in Pa'ia. She worried about going too long without checking on things. Unfortunately, the neighbor accosted her the minute she pulled into her driveway. "We're having an HOA meeting on Saturday to address the street parking. It's simply getting out of hand. I know you've got a lot going on, but I hope you'll be there," she urged. "We need every vote."

Julie Allwood was a great neighbor, but she'd never encountered anyone so enamored with rules, especially when it came to unauthorized cars on the street. "I'm not sure you've noticed, but Mr. Brown's teens had a party last week and there were so many vehicles lining this road that an emergency vehicle would be hard-pressed to pass, if needed." Ms. Allwood placed her hand on Christel's shoulder. "First, it's parking, then it'll migrate to not bringing in recycle bins and painting the fences red. We need you," she implored. "This is important."

Christel held up her hands in surrender. "I'll do my best."

Yeah, just add that to the mountain of things on her plate. All the legal or financial aspects of Pali Maui fell to her, and those responsibilities had nearly overwhelmed her lately. Especially with all that had to be done to deal with her dad's passing.

She glanced at her watch before sliding into her desk chair. Her meeting with the estate attorney was in twenty minutes.

Before Christel had a chance to settle in and review her incoming emails, she was interrupted when Katie popped her head inside her office door. "Hey, we have an issue with the tour this morning. Our new driver failed to show."

"Again?" Christel rolled her eyes in disgust. "Look, I'm drawing up termination papers and he's gone."

Her sister sunk onto the sofa near the window. "Don't you think we should wait and see what excuse he has before we jump to that extreme? Maybe Vic had a family emergency."

Christel shook her head. "Two weeks ago, he was late because his brother's goats got out and he had to help chase them down. Earlier this week, his mom woke up with pink eye and he called in because he was the only one who could take her to the doctor. On Wednesday, the plumbing at his house stopped up." She stared at Katie. "We don't need any more excuses. We need dependability."

Katie nodded. "Yeah, I suppose you're right. I just hate that we've had four people in that position in as many weeks. Now, I have to train someone else." She frowned. "Hiring a new driver isn't going to remedy our current issue. What about right now? We have a parking lot of people gathered and expecting to climb on a tour bus in fifteen minutes and I have a shipment of men's golf shirts being delivered. I don't dare miss being there to sign for the shipment. Last time, the count was off. And not by a little." She glanced at her watch. "I also promised Jon I'd help with a luncheon for fifteen that has been on the books for weeks. Jon plans on debuting a new mahi-mahi dish."

"Well, I'm not sure what we're going to do. I can't drop everything and cover. I have a meeting in a few minutes," Christel told her, checking her watch a second time.

Mig stopped outside her office doorway. "What's up?"

Katie stood. "We don't have a tour driver this morning."

Mig rubbed the top of his head. "Well, you can't just pull someone off the conveyor line. I'll do it."

Relief flooded Katie's face. "Oh, thanks, Mig. I really appreciate it."

Miguel Nakamoa was their farm manager and directed most of the growing operations. He'd been with Pali Maui for longer than Christel could remember. He and his daughter Kala were like family. No one was more dependable.

"Yes, thanks," she told him, adding to Katie's expression of appreciation. "You're a lifesaver, Mig."

"No problem," he told them. "Got it covered." Before turning to leave, he paused. "How's your mother this morning?"

Christel gathered a couple of pens off the top of her desk and placed them back in the container at the side of her Mac. "She's still not sleeping much. I guess that's to be expected."

Mig's eyes filled with sympathy. "Yes, it's difficult to wake up and find the other side of the bed empty. Easier to crouch in a chair with a blanket, and that doesn't provide good rest."

His own wife had left him years ago, when Kala was only seven. Despite the number of years that had passed, he continued to bring her name up more than occasionally. "She was a plate-thrower," he claimed, arguing that he was better off without her. Even so, they all knew Mig had been crushed to find his wife had fallen for someone else. Someone so special, the new relationship warranted abandoning her husband and only child.

"Look, I don't mean to be pushy, but I have a meeting in a few...a very important meeting." She pointed to her watch. "I need time to prepare. So, shoo...both of you."

The estate attorney, Walt Bithell, showed up right on time. Christel spent over three hours with Walt assessing what her father's death meant to the business and all that had to be done. There were corporate and tax issues to resolve. Loan agreements that needed to be revisited. They would have to amend corporate records and file required transactional papers with the state and county. Pali Maui was a huge operation and none of this would be an easy task.

Thankfully, upon her strong urging, her father and mother had both recently updated their wills. A bypass trust had been effectuated at that time. All of her father's assets would now pass to her mother without severe tax consequences. When her mother was gone, the family business would remain intact with ownership conveying in whole to Christel and her siblings.

They were about to conclude the meeting when Walt turned to her. "That wraps everything up except for one outstanding issue."

Christel took a sip of coffee out of the mug on her desk, only to find the liquid inside had turned cold. She wrinkled her nose and pushed the mug aside. "What issue?"

Walt withdrew a folder from his briefcase. "Our paralegal updated the asset search and a found real property that was not on our original inventory. A house in Hana."

Christel scowled. "A house in Hana?"

He nodded. "Here's the property records." He handed the file to her.

She perused the documents inside, studying them carefully. Walt was right. Her father had purchased a house nearly six months earlier. The strange thing was that title was free and clear and held in his name alone.

Walt gave her a thoughtful look. "As you can see, the property is not included in the trust and will pass outside what we set up. Since the asset wasn't specifically addressed in either the trust or the will, you should discuss the disposition with your mother and siblings. Of course, you can elect to retain the property but we'll have to prepare conveyance documents to transfer ownership. You have some time to do that. I recommend the earlier, the better. We can't close the estate until all the assets are disposed of."

Christel nodded her understanding. "Thank you, Walt. I'll look into this." She tucked the file away in her desk drawer and walked him out to his car, thanked him, and bid him goodbye.

After returning to her office, she opened the desk drawer, retrieved the property file and looked over the papers again. Why would her father buy a house in Hana? A rental, perhaps? But that didn't make much sense from an investment perspective. Few tourists rented in Hana when visiting the island. Occupancy demand was far greater in the Ka'anapali area or Lahaina, even Kihei.

Funny, he hadn't told her he'd made this purchase. He certainly had no obligation to address his personal financial interests with her, yet he'd often included her in those discussions and listened carefully to her advice before making decisions. At the very least, she'd have advised moving the asset into the trust. The tax obligation could have been avoided.

Another puzzling notion was that her mother's name was noticeably missing on the deed. A mystery she intended to get to the bottom of. She couldn't explain why exactly, but something on Walt's face when he told her about the house felt a bit off, like there was more he wanted to say. Likely, he had the same questions that had formed in her mind.

Christel got up and dumped the cold coffee, refilled her mug using the thermos on her desk.

She leaned against the back of her credenza and took a sip.

Her dad was on his way back from Hana when he had the accident. Were the two related somehow?

Until she understood more, perhaps it was best to keep this discovery to herself and not tell the others, especially her mother…at least for now.

5

Ava could barely remember the last time she'd slept through the night. The empty bed beside her made it impossible to rest without waking. In fact, she'd lost her appetite and had lost pounds she didn't need to drop. There were times she had trouble focusing, times when she felt despair closing in. This, she supposed, was grief.

She wasn't the sort of woman to wallow. It was time to move on.

In fact, it was time she sent her daughter home. There was no longer a need for Christel to stay at the house to watch over her, making sure she was emotionally stable.

Life had changed forever, but nothing would be gained by remaining mired in self-pity. Instead, she'd bury herself in what gave her a sense of security...her work.

Early the following morning, she donned a pair of jeans and a worn T-shirt. She parked one of Lincoln's baseball caps on her head and went out to the equipment shed. There, she climbed on board a tractor, and carefully maneuvered it out the wide doors, and drove it to the edge of the area where they'd planted coffee beans. The bank bordering the tiny lot had become overgrown with buffelgrass and jimsonweed. Left unmanaged, the weeds would soon overtake the tender new Moka coffee plants.

When she finished plowing, she exchanged the tractor for the loader and scooped the excavated material into a pile where she started a small controlled burn. The smoke brought Mig running.

"Ava, what are you doing?" he asked, looking alarmed.

She explained. "I'm ridding the berms of weeds."

Their farm manager pulled off his glove and rubbed the top of his head. "We have employees who could do that," he suggested. "People we pay to do that."

She leaned against the handle of a shovel and peered at the hedgerows spaced about twelve feet apart. "No worries, Mig. Got it handled."

She worked several more hours, finishing up with a project that she'd wanted to get to for some time. The fence on either side of the loading docks needed a coat of paint. She obliged and gave it to them. Three coats for good measure.

After that, she swept the path leading to her house, noting that her own flower beds could use some attention. Tomorrow, she told herself.

Exhausted but feeling good about all she'd accomplished, Ava took a shower. She combed her neck-length brown hair into place and brushed a little blush across her cheeks. She applied mascara and a sheer lip gloss, then stepped back to take a look in the mirror. She could almost hear her husband's voice. "Well, look at you!" She could almost feel his arms go around her waist and sense him pull her against him, the heat of his breath on her neck.

Unsettled, she shook off the imaginary notion, forced a weak smile, and headed downstairs.

Before leaving, she made her way over to the building

where the offices were housed and alerted Christel she was going to drive over to Alani's.

Her oldest daughter looked up from her Mac. "You need someone to go with you?"

There it was again—that blanket attitude that by losing her husband she was now a mental toddler. "No, I'm good," she assured Christel. "And I don't know when I'll be home, so don't hang around waiting. You have a life. Go live it."

She wandered over to the store and found Katie. Her younger daughter was standing behind the counter, wiping the glass with cleaner and a soft cloth. "I'm going to spend the rest of the day with Alani," she told her.

Katie's face immediately brightened. "Oh, good. That'll do you good, Mom."

Fighting the urge to launch into another speech where she declared herself to be just fine, instead, Ava gave Katie a weak smile. "Have a good day, sweetheart."

"You too, Mom."

As she reached the door, Ava turned. "You haven't seen your brother lately?"

Katie stored the cleaning materials in a cupboard behind the counter. "Which one?"

"Shane. I haven't seen him in days. And my texts go unanswered. Not that it's unusual. He rarely gets back to me quickly," she said.

Katie shrugged. "I think he's been hanging with some friends and fishing over near La Perouse Bay. Jon featured the Kanpachi Shane caught yesterday and served it with caramelized Maui onions. The entrée was a huge hit."

"What about his classes?"

"I think he's good, Mom. At least he said so." Katie gave her a patient look before shooing her out the door. "Quit worrying about him, Mom. At some point he's got to grow up. He's not going to do that with all of us hovering over him and his choices."

Ava knew what Katie said was true. Shane was the baby of the family. She and Lincoln had made the decision not to have any more children after Aiden, but an oops gifted them with a little pudgy-faced kid with the deepest dimples she'd ever seen. Sure, she'd spoiled him some. In part because Lincoln was so hard on him. He seemed to favor Aiden and rarely granted his younger son attention. The issue had been a point of contention between them for a number of years.

Now that Shane was twenty-three and attended college, he did need to show a little more independence. He wanted freedom but didn't always embrace the responsibility that came along with it.

"Okay, well...I'm leaving. Alani has a big luau tonight and her buffet manager is suffering a migraine. I'm going to see what I can do to help her out."

Alani Kané was the sister Ava never had. They'd been barely in their twenties when they met at a birthing class. They were both pregnant for the first time, Alani with twins...Ori and Mia. They'd shared those nine months holding one another's hopes and fears.

She admired Alani. When her friend was young, Alani taught herself to cook, putting herself through school by working in restaurants located in the string of resorts lining Ka'anapali, Kapalua and Napili Beaches. Now, she owned her own luau company—*Te Au Kané*—located beachside not far from Wailea Seaside Church, where her husband, Elta, pastored.

Alani and Ava had much in common, not the least the fact they juggled running a business with the demands of parenting. In fact, she and Alani had made a personal agreement to watch over each other's children if ever the need arose. The kids were no longer minors, but the commitment remained. The Briscoes and Kanés were tight-knit extended family.

As Ava walked across the parking lot, her spirits rose with each step. It felt good to be out of the house, a woman on a mission. Her mission was to quit wallowing. Helping Alani today was another step forward.

Halfway to the beach, Ava stopped and looked out past the pretty manicured lawns to the Pacific, where a couple of kids on paddleboards made their way out to the underwater reef located at the end of the rocky peninsula. A whale-watching boat emerged in the distance, a mere speck on the horizon.

Despite the late afternoon hour, the sun was high and bright, the air almost balmy. She walked a pathway lined with hibiscus bushes full of yellow and pink blooms.

"There you are!" Alani waved in the distance. She wore a signature *muumuu* in a bright-colored floral print. A matching bloom was tucked in her hair behind her ear. "I've been waiting for you all day."

Ava laughed at her. "Oh no! All day?"

Alani reached for her arm and pulled her along. "I think I bit off more than I can chew this time, Ava. Two hundred people, on top of our usual crowd? Ah...what was I thinking?"

Alani was an ambitious businesswoman. No doubt she'd considered the profit possibility in taking on a luau of that size. Of course, she had counted on the help of her buffet manager to pull off an event of this size.

Te au Kané was one of the most sought-after attractions on the island. Tourists paid high amounts for tickets and booked months in advance to experience the quintessential tropical affair. Hula dancers in grass skirts and coconut bras bending and swaying to a four-piece band's music. Smiling people in their finest aloha wear sitting together at tables with Mai Tai drinks in hand with little umbrellas and plates of kalua pork and pineapple rice in front of them. A performer on stage twirling a torch lit at both ends to an urgent drumbeat. A pig baked in an underground imu all day, creating succulent results. And shows that were fast-paced and exciting. A luau was one of the most touristy things to do, and Alani made sure hers never disappointed, even to the point of serving as emcee herself.

Ava and Alani spent the next hours in the kitchen, chopping fresh salmon, tomatoes, and onions for the lomi lomi. They prepared the taro root for specially made poi, a dish Ava never really cared for. She thought it tasted a lot like flour paste. They sliced what seemed like mountains of fresh fruit—pineapple, banana, mangos and passionfruit. The cooks stood over long stainless-steel counters preparing mahi-mahi and ginger teriyaki flank steak that would later be grilled and served hot to the guests. Kalua pork would be a featured dish when the whole pig was unburied from the imu and chopped into tender pieces.

The time spent busy was good for Ava. The opportunity for a prolonged chat with her best friend was even more essential to her soul.

"So, tell me," her friend asked as she peeled a mango. "How are the kids...really?"

Ava sighed. "They're good, I think. I mean, as good as can be expected. They are all hurting, and will be for some time, I'm sure. But they are resilient. Christel is moving back to her own place. Frankly, it's felt a bit crowded having her look over my emotional shoulder every few minutes. She meant well, but... yeah, I'm glad she's heading back home."

Alani sliced a kiwi. "I can only imagine."

Ava reached for a banana and pulled back the peel. "Katie is a lot like me, I suppose. She buries herself in whatever task is at hand. She obsesses over all the details of that restaurant, making sure the linens are all pressed just so, that the food is plated properly, that the menu items are rotated to coincide with whatever fresh fare is available."

Alani slowly shook her head. "Must drive Jon a bit crazy."

Ava laughed slightly. "Oh, yes. Those two. There couldn't be two people more opposite. For as acutely focused on detail as my daughter has always been, Jon is just the opposite. He goes with the flow and rarely worries. I think he balances her beautifully. I also know they can butt heads at times. Jon, smart man that he is, lets Katie win most battles."

Alani chuckled. "Ah, yes...he's a good man. A smart man." Alani lifted her bowl of fruit and moved it to a place in the massive walk-in cooler. She called over her shoulder. "You hungry?"

"I should be, I suppose. But not really. Can't have anything to do with the fact I keep taste testing." She popped a piece of banana inside her mouth.

Alani closed the cooler door and fastened the handle closed. "I'd never let an employee get away with that, you know," she teased.

"Fire me," Ava shot back. "That, or fix me a Mai Tai and send me out to the beach to watch the surfers."

Alani grinned at her. "Well, I'm the boss, and I say it's time for a break. No alcoholic drinks though. I don't want my help pooping out on me."

Ava nudged shoulders with her friend. "Speak for yourself. I can hold my liquor."

"Says the girl who passes out after two cocktails."

Ava lifted her brows. "What exactly is your point?"

Alani took her friend by the elbow and guided her outside. First, she grabbed a tablecloth and a couple of poke bowls along with some chopsticks. "You might not be hungry, but I am."

As they spread the cloth on the sand and sat, it was Ava's turn to check on her friend. "So, what's been on your mind. I can tell you're a bit distracted. And it's not just the big event tonight."

That was the kind of friendship they shared, a relationship built on years and so much time spent together, they could nearly read each other's minds, or at least their moods.

"I'm worried about Mia," Alani confided. She gazed out over the water where dozens of boats now bobbed in the waves. Concern permeated her face. "She's going through something. I even caught her crying the other day. Yet she will not spill and tell me what's wrong."

Ava turned her attention on her friend. "Oh, Alani. I'm so sorry. I've been so wrapped up in my own stuff, well—"

Alani quickly shook her head. "No, stop. The good Lord knows, you had plenty to deal with."

"So, you have no idea what might be prompting those tears?"

Her friend traced the outline of a flower on her muumuu with her finger. "I really don't. It's just...well, she's been pretty distant lately. Even before that, I sensed something was bothering her." She shook her head. "Moms. We know."

"We sure do," Ava agreed.

Alani reached and patted Ava's leg. "But it'll work out. Like Elta said, we may be unaware of the details, but the Lord knows. Our daughter is under His care."

Ava took one of the poke bowls, pulled the plastic lid from the top, and handed it to Alani, then picked up her own. Using chopsticks, she dug for a chunk of raw salmon marinated in soy, onions, and brown sugar. "It's much more difficult to be the mother of grown children. When they're toddlers, you know where they are and have some level of control over what they eat, when they sleep, who they play with. All that goes out the window when they are grown." She popped the salmon into her mouth.

They both sat quietly looking over the ocean for several

seconds before Ava continued. "My kids seem to have weathered the loss of their father. At least, it seems so. They're tough and have pushed through the hurt. From what I can tell, each of them is returning to their normal lives. Or, at least, the new normal."

"That's good to hear." Alani took a bite of avocado. "Emotionally healthy, in fact."

"Yeah, Katie is as busy as ever. I swear, that girl's perfectionist streak is going to be the end of her. I think she likes having a very full plate, if you want to know the truth. She's expanding the retail side and has ordered in a new line of apparel. There's talk of tearing down a wall and adding square footage to the store. I'm really proud of what she's done, nearly on her own. The P&Ls show a growing profit margin."

"But she's still involved in the restaurant too?"

"Oh, yes. *No Ka Oi* has a month-long waiting list for reservations. Especially after *Conde Nast* did a feature in their travel magazine. Jon is a superb chef. Amazing, really. But he's not very business-minded. That is where Katie shines. They butt heads often, but they're a team. A successful team, at that."

Alani let out a laugh. "Ah, I get that. Elta and I are two ends of the pineapple. I'm the crown and like to sprout new leaves. He's the base and likes to dig his slips deep into the dirt and nestle there. Change does not come easily to my man." She looked across at Ava. "Oh, honey. I'm sorry. I wasn't thinking."

Ava quickly brushed the apology aside with an impatient wave. "No, please. Don't try to protect me. I really want...well, I want normal. I miss normal," she murmured, uncomfortable saying it. She paused for a moment, gathering her strength. "Lincoln is gone. There's nothing I can do to alter that. I can only tuck him inside my heart and move forward. I have Pali Maui to run. I have children and grandchildren to support, both emotionally and financially. I never thought I'd have to do it all alone, but that's exactly what I face." She drew a deep breath, trying to dredge up the right words—something that might properly convey her determined attitude. "I simply can't afford to sink into despair, Alani. I don't have a choice."

Ava reached for her best friend's hand. Sometimes holding on was all you could do.

6

Aiden Briscoe woke determined to ignore the leaking shower that needed to be fixed. Instead, he quickly straightened the covers and headed into his tiny bathroom, where he ran a toothbrush over his teeth, washed his face and pulled on a pair of boardshorts. In the kitchen, he downed a quick cup of coffee, then grabbed an apple and wedged it in his teeth as he tucked his snorkel gear under his arm and headed out.

A rooster scurried across the sidewalk in front of him as he made his way the few blocks to Canal Street, where his uncle ran a charter business for tourists wanting to take a snorkeling or whale watching excursion.

"*Aloha*," he said as he neared a shopkeeper who had finished sweeping the sidewalk in front of his store. Aiden paused to hold the door open for him.

The man smiled. "*Mahalo*," he said as a thank you. "*Aloha*." He waved as Aiden moved on.

The tiny town of Lahaina was known as a historic village that had been transformed into a Maui hotspot with dozens of art galleries and a variety of unique shops and restaurants.

Lahaina was also where Aiden currently called home, having nabbed a small thirteen-hundred-square-foot single-story on Waine'e Street a couple of years back.

The house needed a lot of work. He'd spent the first year tearing up moldy orange shag carpet and pulling down wood paneling from the walls. His parents thought he was nuts.

"The electrical is outdated, son. Looks dangerous," his dad warned.

His mother had nodded in agreement. "Honey, I want to be happy for you. Really, I do. I'm afraid this place will be nothing more than a money pit. Come home," she urged. "Move back to Pali Maui and save some money toward a bigger down payment. When it's time, we'll help you out when you find something...nicer. We'll lend financial support." She'd looked to his dad. "In fact, we could do that now, couldn't we, Lincoln?"

Aiden had known it was past time he got out on his own. While he loved both of them dearly, he didn't need their blessing and didn't want their advice. And he didn't want their money.

His salary from Maui Emergency Management was nothing to brag about, but the income was sufficient to secure a loan. Despite that, the purchase had strapped him financially, which meant most of the renovation had to be done as additional funds became available in his budget and when he had the time. He hadn't had a lot of either.

When he did have spare time, he'd spend the hours working on house projects. Not today. Today he had to get away and clear his head. The past weeks had been pretty gnarly. There hadn't been a night since his dad died that Aiden didn't wake in a cold sweat trying to erase images of the accident.

In an attempt to keep his mind fully occupied, he'd stayed as busy as possible, which prompted the guys down at the department to press him to take some time off. "We can manage, bro," they told him. Leaving no room for argument,

Aiden simply responded, "Nah, I'm better off working right now."

He didn't need the empty headspace filling with those nightmare scenes—the mangled metal at the bottom of the ravine, the exploded airbag straining through broken glass windows. His inability to save the man he loved most on this earth.

The fact his dad was gone.

The burden he carried was heavy and one he kept hidden deep inside. He would take all that to his grave.

"Aiden, my boy!" His uncle's gravelly voice mingled with the sound of a boat motor and the chatter of tourists excited to embark on their date with adventure. "You ready to go out? The sea is calling our name."

Aiden pointed his thumb in the direction of a group down the way who were waiting to load onto a waiting catamaran. "Who's taking the charter this morning?"

"I talked ole Sam into covering for me." His uncle rubbed his tanned belly poking out from his open short-sleeved shirt. He let out a loud laugh, nearly cackling. "Even Captain Jack needs some time off once in a while."

The locals had nicknamed his mother's only brother Santa of the Sea, and for good reason. Not only did he sport a big belly, but he hadn't shaved in years, resulting in a long gray beard hanging well below his chin. His face was ruddy from time spent in the sun and he had puffy cheeks the size of small apples.

Captain Jack didn't embrace the philosophy held by dentists that one must brush daily. His lack of using a toothbrush had cost him a couple of teeth. The vacant spots in his dental structure only served to bolster his booming voice. Yet he was anything but jolly. In fact, his gruff nature seemed to scare young children until they caught his true spirit—which was as soft as a marshmallow. Many people on the island had been beneficiaries of his generosity, financial and otherwise, and always anonymously.

"I'm looking forward to spending some time with my favorite nephews," his uncle said waving him onto the hard-bottom inflatable vessel that had been originally designed for search and rescue missions for the U.S. Coast Guard. The raft was powered by a computerized four-stroke engine and was certified for twenty-four passengers. "Climb in."

Aiden tossed his snorkel gear into the bottom of the boat. "Nephews? Is Shane coming with us?"

"Your brother is my new summer hire. Your mom thought he could use some gainful employment while on break from school." His uncle frowned as he checked his watch. "Nephew, or no, if that kid doesn't show up in the next five minutes, he's gonna be outta work before he even begins."

On cue, Shane came running from the direction of Banyan Tree Park. The banyan, with its dangling vines and twelve connected trunks, was a Lahaina landmark. "Sorry I'm late," his brother shouted. Upon approach, he stopped and leaned over with his hands on his knees, breathless. "Crowd traffic...held me up."

Uncle Jack waved off his excuse. "Eh, was that her name?"

Shane's eyes twinkled as he looked up into his uncle's face. "Cindy," he admitted.

"Get in the raft," Jack growled, but not before Aiden caught the slight smile peeking from behind his unkempt beard.

Shane and Aiden climbed aboard and sunk onto one of the bench seats as their uncle launched the massive raft. They exchanged their flip-flops for fins and checked the straps on their face masks as the vessel eased from the dock. As soon as they'd cleared the no-wake zone, Uncle Jack pulled down on the throttle. The engine roared to life and swept them across the water, catching speed until the sun-warmed wind rushed against Aiden's face.

More than once, Aiden had been out on a charter filled with tourists when his uncle leaned and patted the side of the inflated boat. "For anyone worried about our rig, let me assure you, this raft is the safest craft on the water. We've even rescued Coast Guard boats in trouble. Yup, Old Grandma has to save the grandchildren once in a while."

There were many reasons Aiden was grateful he lived on Maui. The ocean, known as Moana to native Hawaiians, ranked high on that list. He lifted his face to catch the fine spray that came as a bold flurry each time the raft traversed a wave. The tide appeared drawn to the horizon, waves rolling in and out, its rhythm as steady as his own heartbeat. Perhaps that was why he felt so soothed here.

Shane turned to face the captain's perch. "So, Unc..." he hollered over the sound of the engine. "We heading across the channel to Lana'i?"

Jack simply nodded before pointing the raft in the direction of an area of towering sea cliffs. No doubt, he intended to take them to his secret secluded cove where often spinner dolphins could be seen next to large green sea turtles. If lucky, a person might catch a glimpse of a monk seal or in very rare cases, an off-season whale.

A short time later, Jack eased close to a black-rocked reef and cut the engine. He stroked his beard. "Well, there you go."

"You coming in with us?" Shane asked.

Jack shook his head. "Not this time." He maneuvered his large frame to the front of the raft and tossed some weighted orange floats alongside the vessel. "I'll hang and enjoy the ohana...watch for mermaids." He winked.

Their uncle was a storyteller. It was a long-standing joke between the crusty man and his nephews that he'd never wed because he was in love with a mermaid.

"Enjoy these early morning conditions while you can," he

told them. "Reports are we'll have some trade winds kicking up this afternoon."

Shane didn't hesitate. He slipped over the side and planted his face in the water. Seconds later, he kicked his flippers and submerged a few feet below the surface.

Aiden did likewise. The underside of the sea never ceased to astound his senses. The views would never get old...the reefs of gold, purple and orange hues scattered with brightly colored fish darting in and out of the rock formations.

He was exploring only a little while before a large *honu* drifted in front of him. Sea turtles were native to Hawaii. The hard-shelled creatures could reach lengths of four feet and weights of over three hundred pounds.

It was his father who taught him all about these majestic creatures. He was only a little boy when he first learned the mottled brown upper shell was called their carapace. The under shell, or plastron, was yellow. Honu mainly ate algae and seagrasses, and their lungs were of a size that allowed the turtles to remain underwater for many hours.

It was his dad who taught him to swim, to face his fear of the water and the creatures below. His dad patiently trained him how to balance on a surfboard, to race down a zipline over top of palms and bougainvillea and how to whip and dunk lures from the shoreline in order to land an aggressive trevally —a golden snapper or a goat fish.

How many hours had he spent with his dad snorkeling the pristine waters surrounding Maui spotting bigeye scad, jacks and needle fish, eels and reef sharks?

Aiden choked back emotion and surfaced, blew to purge his snorkel tube of water.

Uncle Jack waved from inside the boat. "Hey, it just came over the radio that there's been a whale spotted only a few feet from the point." He pointed.

Every year during the winter months, over ten thousand

humpbacks annually migrated to the warm, shallow waters of Maui and created thunderous splashes and aerial performances that kept tourists in awe. The whales particularly loved the Auau Channel, the shallow area between West Maui, Lana'i, and Moloka'i, and known to be one of the most popular whale breeding grounds in Hawaii.

It wasn't often a whale would be spotted out of season, even this close to Lana'i.

Aiden gave his uncle a thumbs-up. He nodded and secured his mask in place, then plummeted down a few feet. His arms swept wide, pushing him through the water. That's when he heard it...the whale song. He stopped and floated in place, listening to a sound so soulful, so mournful, that the notes pierced his own emotions.

Aiden had trained for rescue, had spent much of his time pulling people from car accidents and dangerous tides, yanking them back from the brink of disaster. Yet, when it mattered the most, he hadn't even had the chance to save his dad.

Unbidden, the full impact of his loss hit him.

Since the accident, Aiden had held everything inside. There would be no more fishing, no ziplines or snorkeling. No more late-night talks or unsolicited advice given. No warnings about bad electrical systems or the need to change the oil in his car regularly. In survival mode, he hadn't allowed himself to feel the enormity of the fact, or what it meant, that his father was forever gone.

He heard the whale song again.

In that moment, he lost control. Emotions rolled over him like hot lava. Right there under the secrecy of the sea, out of the sight of others, he finally let it all go.

He wept.

7

After work, Katie returned home to find a message on their answering machine from Willa's middle school reporting she'd been absent from afternoon classes. They didn't find a permission slip on record.

Katie groaned. First, she couldn't figure out why the school administration continued to use her home phone number instead of her cell, despite numerous requests both in writing and in person. Second, she needed to bring the issue up again with Jon. There was no reason to have a landline when each of them carried their cell phones. It was an unnecessary expense, and it created situations like the one with the school. Third, this was the second time Willa had skipped classes. Guaranteed, it would be the last.

She straightened her shoulders and marched up the stairs, past the open bathroom door—a bathroom cluttered with towels on the floor and a counter covered with mascara wands and tall cans of hairspray. Katie flung open her daughter's bedroom door. "Willa! We need to talk."

The room was empty.

Katie huffed and swung around. "Willa!" she hollered.

Downstairs, the door opened, and laughter drifted up the stairs, the animated voices of her husband and oldest daughter. Katie darted down the stairs.

"Where have you been?" she demanded, not bothering to tone down her displeasure.

Jon lifted his eyebrows in surprise. He leaned and kissed her forehead. "Hey, babe. What's up?"

Katie glanced between Willa and Jon, who was holding little Noelle. "Are you letting her eat candy? It's less than an hour before dinner time." She pulled the sticky sucker from her tiny daughter's dimpled fists, sending the toddler into a fit of tears.

Katie drew a deep, impatient breath and reached for the crying little girl. At the same time, she directed her attention to her older daughter. "Willa, the school called. You missed classes."

Willa looked up at Jon. "I know, but Dad—"

Jon pulled his sunglasses from the top of his tousled brown hair. "I went and got her."

Katie drew back, pulled her brows into a frown. "Went and got her?"

Jon made a funny face at his baby daughter, which immediately stopped her from crying. "Yeah, your Uncle Jack called from the boat. He and your brothers were out at Lana'i and spotted a whale. Out of season. He urged me to grab the girls and said he'd meet us at the dock and take them out so they could spot her. She was even breaching. He told me to bring my SeaLife Micro so we could get some good shots." Her husband shook his head and smiled at Noelle, who held out her arms for him. He took her from Katie. "You should have seen it, babe."

Katie drew her hands into fists at her side. "Okay, let me get this straight. You pulled our daughter out of school to go see a whale? Without checking in with me?"

Jon shrugged, gave Willa a wink. "Well, yeah. I did call you. I even texted."

Katie pulled her phone from her pocket and stared at the alerts. She must've missed them while she was reorganizing the shelves in the back room at *No Ka 'Oi*. Jon and the kitchen staff always left things a mess. Who stored freshly picked papayas inside cooking pans? She'd purchased baskets for that.

Jon grinned at her. "See? I did tell you."

His charm failed to sway her. "The office said they had no record of permission." She nodded in the direction of the message machine as if to buoy up her argument.

"That's silly. I didn't just walk in and kidnap our daughter."

Willa ran her fingers through her long, dark hair, tugging when necessary to untangle the natural curls. "Gosh, Mom. You know those ladies in the office are all emos. They thrive on drama, even if they have to conjure some up."

Katie admonished her daughter with a stern look. "Don't talk about your elders with disrespect."

Willa rolled her eyes. Katie could have sworn she caught Jon doing the same before he turned away and focused on putting Noelle down. The minute the toddler was free from his arms, she charged across the floor to where their dog rested on the carpet and flung herself on top of him. He yelped.

"Careful, Noelle. Don't hurt him," Willa cautioned her little sister.

Givey was a mixed breed Cavapoo—part Cavalier Charles Spaniel and part poodle—a gift from Jon to make up for neglecting to make the insurance payment. Twice.

The following day, he thrust the adorable mutt into her arms and told her the dog's name was Forgive—Givey, for short. And, yes...she'd forgiven Jon, as always, but she still took over their personal finances, relieving him of the duty.

Katie pulled in her irritation, but only slightly. "Okay, here's the deal." She pointed at Willa. "No more skipping classes for any reason without *my* permission." She turned to Jon. "Understood?"

He simply grinned that smile that had pierced her heart the minute she met him. "Yeah. No problem." He grabbed her and pulled her into an embrace. In order to further tease her, he rubbed his scruffy cheek alongside her own. "Whatever the missus says."

Before she could argue, he planted a kiss on her lips. She let herself enjoy his romantic gesture for several seconds before she attempted to pull back, knowing the girls were watching. He wouldn't let her. Instead, he playfully tightened his hug.

Katie grabbed his arms and pushed him back. "Okay, okay. The girls—"

In response, Jon let loose. He reached and pinched Katie's bottom as he turned to his daughters. "Ladies, I must ask—have you ever, in this entire island, seen a woman as beautiful as my gal?"

Willa shook her head in feigned disgust. "Get a room, you two."

Little Noelle simply giggled and planted her face in Givey's golden fur. "Get a *woom*," she repeated.

8

Ava sat across the desk from Christel. "What do you mean, your dad bought a house?"

Her daughter threw her a look that clearly indicated she'd rather be anywhere else. "I'm sorry, Mom. I don't have a lot of information more than this." She slid a document across the desk.

Ava picked up the single page and examined it. "A deed." She quickly scanned the contents. "In his name only." She looked up, confused. "I don't understand."

Christel's only answer was a gentle shrug of one shoulder.

Ava swallowed hard, trying to assimilate the information. "Where did you get this?" she demanded. Realizing her tone was far too harsh, she tempered her reaction and quickly added, "This is all so confusing."

"The estate attorney." Christel's face filled with sympathy. There was no doubt the situation had surprised her daughter as well. "Walt was pulling together a list of assets and doing due diligence when he found this parcel of real estate. As you might note from the date on the deed, Dad bought it less than two months ago."

"I see that," Ava said, frowning. She tossed the deed back on the desk. "Why would he need a house in Hana?" The words were no more out of her mouth than the thought dawned, as it had no doubt in her daughter's mind as well. "He was on his way back from Hana."

Christel nodded. "Yes."

Ava stood and paced the room. "None of this makes sense." Her scrambled thoughts drifted to the scene outside her daughter's office window, where the lane leading to the guest parking area was lined with hibiscus, birds of paradise, and pink ginger. She remembered planting that bedding area years ago when she'd first moved to Pali Maui. The task had blistered her hands, and Lincoln had shown up offering a pair of gardening gloves. "You might want to use these," he told her. "Those hands are far too pretty to scratch up."

She'd considered his remark a bit sexist at the time. While she'd argued over similar comments many times, the look he gave her as he lifted her to her feet caused her to hold her tongue. The kiss that followed melted away any criticism she wished to convey.

That was Lincoln's manner. He had a way of charming her that dislodged her sensibilities.

Ava gazed beyond the parking area to the packing house. She folded her arms tightly against her chest. "You know, the packing house and those shipping docks were all that were here when your grandfather bought this place."

Robert Hart was a successful cardiac surgeon and Pearl Harbor history buff. Being fascinated with the Hawaiian islands, Ava's father bought the faltering pineapple operation on Maui as a tax write-off. Their family was living in San Francisco then. Ava was sixteen when her mother, Esther, died of cancer. In the aftermath, her heartbroken father picked her and her sister, Vanessa, up and moved them here to Maui. Likely, he was trying to escape the pain of his loss.

Sadly, she now fully understood that kind of loss, the wanting to uproot your life, change everything in order to make sense of tragedy. Since Lincoln's accident, everywhere she looked, memories attacked her heart. She would like nothing more than to find a way to escape the pain. Yet she had responsibilities, a life here. People depended on her.

"Mom, do you think Dad was keeping secrets from you?" The question was straightforward. It deserved a forthright answer.

"No, I do not." And yet, something deep in her heart was cracking open. Did Lincoln keep secrets?

The ground beneath her feet was suddenly unstable.

Ava swiped at a sudden runaway tear. "I was barely sixteen when we came here. Your grandfather soon discovered he was not as good at running a full-time business operation as he was at fixing myocardial infarctions and septal defects in arteries. He tired of profit and loss statements and growing projections and never-ending paperwork." Ava ran her fingers through the side of her hair, remembering. "He turned the operation over to me and went back to practicing medicine. I was barely eighteen at the time."

"I—I didn't realize you were so young, Mom." Christel leaned back in her chair. "That was a lot of pressure for someone who was barely an adult. What about Aunt Vanessa?"

Ava shrugged. "She had already left for the mainland to pursue her dreams. When my father suffered his stroke and died, Pali Maui became fully mine. She wanted nothing to do with any of it."

Ava turned and looked at her oldest daughter. "Lincoln and I poured our hearts and many hours into building Pali Maui into the successful operation it is now, while concurrently raising you children."

The history of this place went unspoken—the sacrifices she and Lincoln had made. Together. Always together.

The early years were lean. It had taken nearly everything she and Lincoln could muster to increase the acreage, to expand and upgrade the processing and packing sheds, and secure adequate distribution. Lincoln worked his charm and they partnered with a shipping company based out of Oahu and began sending produce internationally. They also soon increased their deliveries to the mainland to twice weekly. It was her idea to invest in advertising, both print and television. After much planning, they strategically built their name and brand until the Pali Maui pineapples were recognized worldwide.

Later years brought expansion into the tourism trade, a retail operation, and the decision to plant small parcels of coffee beans, mangoes, papayas and bananas. The landscaping was upgraded until the entire acreage boasted a lush park-like atmosphere that showcased trees and plants native to the islands, a large gazebo, and a number of ponds with strolling paths.

They renovated the residential house and built offices and additional housing for their farm manager, Miguel and his family, as well as homes they hoped their adult children would someday utilize.

As revenues continued to increase, they added a small golf course on the far side of the hill and a restaurant that served farm-fresh fare and freshly caught island fish. The restaurant soon showed up in luxury travel guides and magazines and was often featured on popular internet blogs.

Together, she and Lincoln had amassed much success by anyone's measure. They had done so via a partnership that extended well beyond marriage. It had taken the best of both of them and a kind of trust few business people could match.

Ava's lip quivered.

Now, this.

Apparently, Lincoln had kept a secret. He'd purchased a

house and hidden the fact. A move that was out of character for her husband. Her stomach quivered slightly. What else didn't she know? What other things had he not told her?

Her eyes darkened. "Do you have the keys?"

Christel raised her eyebrows. "Keys?"

Ava patiently repeated herself. "Do you have the keys?" She paused, pulled in a breath. "To the house."

Christel nodded and pulled a desk drawer open. She retrieved a small plain manila envelope. "Here. There's only one key, and it's inside."

Ava stiffened. She reached for the envelope and took it from her daughter's hand.

"What are you going to do?" Christel asked.

Ava turned the envelope over. She opened the fastener on the flap and shook out the contents into her open palm. After letting the empty envelope drop to the floor, she held up the single key and stared at it before answering.

"First thing tomorrow morning, I'm going to get up and take a shower, drink a cup of coffee, and eat breakfast. Like always, I'm going to have my morning meeting with Mig and go over anything that needs my attention." Ava straightened her shoulders, lifted her chin. "After that, I'm going to drive to Hana and check out this new house of mine."

9

Katie climbed the bleachers and handed Christel her skinny caramel macchiato made with coconut milk. "Sorry I'm late. The drive-up line at Starbucks was backed up."

Christel took the coffee drink. "No problem. Thanks for picking it up."

Katie nodded in the direction of the ball field. "Who's ahead?"

Christel lifted the lid from her coffee and took a sip. "The boys' team is down by two."

While the Briscoe siblings all led extremely busy lives, they made every effort to gather occasionally for breakfast, often catching the dawn league games both of the guys were involved in.

"Aw, c'mon!" Aiden hollered from the dugout. "I've seen better swings on a porch."

Katie rolled her eyes. "I hope he has his sphygmomanometer in his truck. His blood pressure goes any higher, and he's going to have to place a cuff around his own arm." She dug in her bag for a banana and peeled the yellow skin back.

"I thought we're going to breakfast after the game?"

Katie shook her head. "Sorry, can't. I'm hoping to have a meeting with Mom later. I think I have her convinced we need to put in a full bakery shop with specialty coffees." She pointed to her sister's coffee. "Do you know how much profit is in one of those? We need to capture that revenue from the tourists that wait to board the tour bus."

"We already serve coffee and donuts."

"Well, sure. Drip coffee and packaged donuts. I'm talking espresso machine and freshly baked almond croissants, pineapple muffins, and crème puffs."

"And who's going to run all that?" she asked with a laugh in her voice. "Your plate is full already. Jon certainly doesn't have time." Christel stood and yelled, "You asleep out there, Blue?"

The umpire shook off her criticism and got back in position as the pitcher wound up for another throw.

"Oh, ye of little faith," Katie chided. She stood as well and cheered as her brothers' team, the Dirtbags, struck out the opposing side and came in off the field a half-hour later winners with the score 7-2.

Shane sidled up next to Katie and gave her a playful hug. "So, Christel says you are bailing on our breakfast date?"

Aiden flung the bat over his shoulder as they headed for the parking lot. "Oh, no. That's not the deal. We're all heading to Charley's."

Christel raised her eyebrows at her sister. "You're not likely going to get out of this one, you know."

"But, Jon—"

"But nothing," Aiden said, linking his arm with hers. "No arguments."

The ball field was located on the outskirts of Pa'ia and was only a short distance from Charley's, a popular bar and restaurant named after a Great Dane dog and where graybeard bikers and young surfers both lined up for the best food and fun around. Willie Nelson claimed Charley's was his kind of place and often played impromptu concerts on the tiny stage anytime he visited the island.

Despite the line at the door, Katie and her siblings were seated right away. The owner was a friend of their family's and a customer. Pali Maui delivered cases of fresh pineapples every morning.

They were seated at a corner booth at the rear of the bustling establishment. Minutes later, a perky young blonde showed up with an order pad and pen. "Hey, what can I get for you?" She turned her smoky brown eyes on Shane and smiled.

He was quick to return the smile. "You're new here."

She nodded. "Yeah. Started yesterday." She flipped her long blonde hair over her shoulder. "Vacationed with college friends. They returned to Chicago, and I decided to stay."

Her little brother was immediately pulled in and said, "We should go out sometime."

Both Christel and Katie looked at Shane with amazement, at his direct approach. He didn't even know her name, though she didn't seem to mind. She laughed and answered, "Sure! I'm Aimee Battista. Here's my phone number." She pulled a page from her order pad and scribbled on it with her pen, then handed the paper over.

"Great! I'll call you."

Katie exchanged looks across the table at Christel. Her older sister made a point of clearing her throat while Aiden tried to hide his amusement.

"Oh! I'm sorry," the young waitress said, apologizing. "What will you all have?"

Aiden folded his menu and handed it to the girl. "Biscuits and gravy, please. Two eggs. Over easy. And a side of bacon." He paused. "With pancakes."

Katie cleared her throat as if choking. "You sure that's enough?"

Aiden laughed her off. "What? I'm hungry."

Christel ordered an omelet. "Hold the hashbrowns."

"I'll eat 'em," Aiden offered.

Katie put in her order for two poached eggs with one slice of toast and a fruit cup. She had to watch her weight. She elbowed Shane, who was still gazing at the girl. "You're up."

"What?" he muttered. "Oh…I'll have scrambled eggs, sausage, and toast."

Aimee wrote their order down and directed a final grin at Shane. "Coming right up," she promised.

Katie watched as her little brother stared at the girl's behind as she walked away. "Hey, Shane. You might not want to be so obvious."

"Yeah," Christel chimed in. "Try diving deeper than the shallow end once in a while."

Shane scratched his shoulder. "I could use some support here, bro. They're ganging up on me," he told Aiden.

Aiden lifted his open palms. "Hey, you're on your own."

Christel drew a deep breath. "Hey, guys. This is as good of a time as any, I suppose. I have to talk to you about something important."

They all gave her their attention. "Yeah, what's up?" Shane asked, reaching for a packet of sugar.

Christel revealed what Walt Bithell had found while assembling the estate assets. She explained the deed, how their father put only his name on the property title and had failed to disclose any of it to their mother. "I told her this morning."

Aiden let his back fall back against the banquette seat. "Wow. What did she say?"

Christel fingered the utensils on the table in front of her. "She was stunned, as you can imagine. So was I."

"A house?" Katie's hand went to her chest. "A rental maybe?" she asked, reaching for some plausible explanation.

Christel shook her head. "There are no indications that is

what Dad intended. We may never really know his purpose. The fact remains, he bought a house. And he didn't tell anyone."

Shane nodded, like he was contemplating that. He cleared his throat. "So, what's Mom going to do?"

Christel fingered her silverware. "She needs answers. As you can imagine, her mind is racing with questions. She has the key and is going to Hana today to check it out."

Aiden nearly knocked over his water glass. "Alone? Absolutely not!"

Christel handed him some napkins. "I urged her to let one of us go with her. She insisted she wanted to do this alone. In the end, I got her to agree to take Alani with her."

Katie let out a breath she hadn't even realized she'd been holding. "I wish you would have told us first...before revealing the fact to Mom, I mean."

"Yeah," Shane said with a frown. "Dad's gone, and this now becomes a one-sister show? I think we all should have been there."

Aiden nodded. "I agree."

Christel glanced around the table, turned impatient. "What would you have said that I didn't?"

"That's not the point," Katie corrected. "This is big. We all should have been there to lend support. At the very least, we should have been told first."

"So Mom could feel ganged up on? I don't see how that would have been better."

Katie clenched her jaw and leaned forward. "We do things as a family, Christel."

Christel folded her arms across her chest, not letting their protests throw her. "Look, I did what I thought was best." She made a move to leave.

Aiden grabbed her arm. "Christel, wait. Don't go charging out. Sit down."

Shane quickly joined his brother and made a plea of his own. "Yeah, c'mon. No need for everyone to get all huffy."

Katie folded her arms and went silent, only granting her sister a small token nod.

Aiden leaned back in his chair. "Going forward, let's agree on something." He looked around the table. "When it comes to Mom and everything she's going through and all she has on her plate moving forward, can we all acknowledge we're in this together?" He shot Christel a look. "All of us...together."

"I don't know why everyone is so upset. I'm including you now," Christel argued.

"Together," the other three repeated, overriding her protest in unison.

Christel lifted her hands in surrender. "Okay, okay. I get it." She paused and looked at her siblings from across the table. "Together."

10

"Are you going to tell me what's going on?" Alani climbed into the passenger side of Ava's car. "Why did I have to drop everything and join you for a road trip? Where are we going?"

From inside the car, Ava shut the driver's door then pressed her finger onto the ignition button on the dash. The engine roared to life. "We're going to Hana."

Her best friend's eyebrows shot up. "Hana? But that drive takes hours, especially up that winding road filled with tourists."

"Which is why we need to get going," Ava explained. "We need to beat the traffic." She pulled her sunglasses from their perch in her hair and positioned them into place. "I had Jon make us some sandwiches...ham and gouda with his homemade bacon jam. They're in the cooler in the back seat. Along with some drinks." She put the car in gear and pulled out. She circled the large brick driveway before maneuvering the vehicle past the offices, the restaurant and retail shop, and down the tree-lined lane in the direction of the highway.

Alani sat quietly with a deep frown on her face as they

made their way down the winding lane. Finally, her friend could take it no longer. "Ava, this is crazy. Why are we going to Hana?"

Ava swallowed and explained what she'd learned. "That's all I know right now, Alani. But I've got to check it out. I didn't want to go alone."

Alani was speechless for a moment. "He didn't tell you? That's not like Lincoln." Her brows drew together. "He doesn't do that."

Ava had thought that as well. "The fact is, he did." Admitting her husband had hidden a purchase of this magnitude pulled at her gut. "I've thought long and hard about all the reasons Lincoln might have had for not disclosing he'd bought a house. Frankly, I've come up with nothing." She paused, letting the unspoken implication hang in the air. "If he intended to purchase an investment property, why Hana? We both know the remote little town at the southern end of the island is not known for prime rental potential. Even if he meant the property as a rental, but from what we can tell, the house remained vacant in the months since closing. There is no record he contacted a rental agency, or even a property management company. That simply doesn't seem to have been his intention."

Ava drummed the steering wheel with her thumbs as she pulled to a stop at the end of the lane. She waited for two cars to pass before pulling onto the highway and driving in the direction of the airport, where she would ultimately turn onto the famous Road to Hana. "Certainly, the house was not going to be a getaway for the two of us. He'd have consulted with me first. If he'd meant it as a surprise, why wait months to tell me?" She slowly shook her head. "And he would know Hana would not ever be my first choice as a vacation escape. The drive is too far, too treacherous."

As she pointed out that reality, Lincoln's accident, no doubt, formed in both of their minds. The women drove in silence for several miles before Alani spoke up. "Maybe he intended it as a gift for one of the children—Shane, perhaps."

Ava turned south at the intersection just before the airport. She gazed across the seat to her friend. "That's not likely. Again, he would have consulted with me."

"Maybe he bought the house to give to someone in need. Lincoln could be generous. Yes, that's it. He meant the purchase as a token of his charity. He always gave immense amounts to the church. I've never seen a man so willing to part with his money any time he became aware of a need," Alani argued, trying to convince them both there was a plausible explanation in all this.

Ava was pretty sure she might have groaned aloud at the idea. "A gift that cost hundreds of thousands? And he didn't tell his wife?"

Alani folded her hands in her ample lap as an unspoken consideration passed between them. "Well, I refuse to believe Lincoln had nefarious intentions. The idea doesn't wash with the man I knew and loved."

Ava let her gaze drift to the ocean shoreline out her driver's window. That, right there, was the reason Ava adored Alani. Unlike some overly zealous churchgoers, the woman sitting across from her actually lived what she believed.

Alani was a fierce advocate. Her friend refused to entertain the worst about anyone, let alone those she loved. A few years back, their church secretary was discovered taking money from the donation box. Despite being caught red-handed, Alani argued the woman must've needed the funds. She asked Elta not to press charges and even offered the thieving secretary a second job working at the luau. Sadly, it came to light that the woman had not simply made an error of judgment but had a history of embezzlement. Even then, Alani urged Elta to consent to a plea agreement that included her returning to the mainland and even helped cover her defense attorney's bill.

Alani was loyal. Plain and simple. Nothing shook that loyalty.

As they drove beyond the town of Pa'ia, the road up the mountain quickly became shaded with tall foliage lining the narrow highway—eucalyptus, kukui nut, bamboo, and lush green tropical plants.

Occasionally, a few residences sprouted out of the thick vegetation. While some were vacation properties with intense views of the ocean, others were shacks with surfboards leaning against the railings on dilapidated porches. Large dogs ran free and barked as cars passed. Widened spots in the highway were packed with tourists who pulled off and parked, wanting to explore breathtaking waterfalls or scenic overlooks. They crossed one-lane bridges, and the winding road was filled with hairpin turns that often caused even people with strong stomachs to feel a bit queasy.

Halfway to their destination was a sideroad to a little village known as Ke'anae. Ava turned to her passenger. "You need to stop for a quick break?"

"Oh my, yes," Alani quickly answered. "I needed to stop miles ago."

"Why didn't you say so?" Ava said as she put on her blinker and slowed.

When they were parked, Alani made her way to the restroom. Ava got out and leaned against the car, taking in the sights. Ke'anae Peninsula and the small village had long been one of Ava's favorite spots on the island. She loved how the ocean tore through jagged lava boulders along the coastline, especially at high tide. The impossibly blue water did something to her soul.

A short while later, Alani hollered from across the parking

area. "Do you want something from Aunt Sandy's?" Even from the distance, Ava could smell the freshly baked banana bread and the other homemade delicacies the roadside food stand was known for.

Ava shook her head no. Minutes later, her friend returned loaded with not only a miniature loaf of banana bread, but she had a kalua pork sandwich in one hand.

"I packed sandwiches," Ava reminded.

"Oh, I know. But I couldn't resist. I like the way they add those little diced onions."

Ava smiled. There was a reason her friend had dimpled elbows. "Well, I might as well pull out our lunch then."

They found a grassy spot near some Hala trees. Ava grabbed the small blanket she'd retrieved from the trunk of her car and spread it out then opened the picnic basket and unloaded the contents, including the sandwiches Jon had made and a small container of pineapple baked beans. Her son-in-law had also tucked in two crème brulee desserts in throwaway containers.

Waves crashed against the shoreline and the air carried the scent of plumeria and rich, moist earth. Ava made a note to break from work and go on excursions more often. Under better circumstances, of course.

"Oh, my goodness!" Alani reached for a plastic spoon. She pulled the lid off the container and dug in. "*Mahalo*," she said before delivering a large scoop to her mouth.

"You're eating dessert first?" Ava questioned.

"Absolutely," Alani told her. "I've learned to not wait for the good stuff." She let out a hefty laugh as she gazed across the horizon. "Oh, Ava. I remember bringing the kids here for picnics when they were little. Mia was fascinated by that old stone church. Said she wanted to grow up and get married there someday." She pointed to the historic structure in the distance, surrounded by tall palm trees jutting into the blue sky. Beyond the rickety fence line, taro fields stretched for acres to the base of the green mountainside. "Where did the years go?"

Ava folded a napkin across her lap. "Lincoln and the boys used to hike down that path to a spot on the lava rock where they'd fish for *ulua*."

Alani took another bite of the crème brulee. "You and the girls didn't fish with them?"

Ava unwrapped her sandwich. "No. We collected limpets off the rocks. Christel was really good at finding them."

"Oh, I love *opihi*. I cook the shells in chili pepper, water, and a bit of shoyu sauce. The dish is one of Elta's favorites." Her gaze drifted to the rocky shoreline. "You know, we lost Mia here once. Terrified both of us. She was only ten."

"Alani, I didn't know that. Every parent's nightmare."

"She'd slipped off when we weren't watching. You know the tiny scar above her right eyebrow?"

Ava pulled up a picture of Mia in her mind. Giant brown eyes on a perfect face. But a scar? No, she had never noticed one.

"We were frantic. As you know, the waves here on the peninsula can be treacherous. We didn't know what had happened to her. Do you know where we found her?"

Ava shook her head.

"Playing in a little tidal pool filled with sea urchins. She'd tumbled off the rocks, landed in a patch of black sand, and said she'd gone into the water to wash off the blood—she knew better—but she wasn't the least bit concerned about the gash over her eye." Alani gazed over at the horizon. "My girl's independent spirit—her *'uhane ku' oko 'a*—often robbed her of good judgment." She shook her head. "As afraid as we were, that day still holds good memories. So many here at Ke'anae Peninsula."

Ava basked in the distraction of the picnic and time spent

with her friend. "Yes. Good memories, indeed. Somehow, I never let myself imagine how things would change."

"Ah." Her friend nodded. "Yes, like it or not, *ho'ololi* always comes."

The two women finished their picnic and loaded back up in the car, drinks in hand. They had less than twenty miles to go before reaching Hana but the route was lined with steep valley walls and extremely narrow spans of roadway, which would slow their travel.

The pavement narrowed even more at switchback turns bordered with guardrails. Ava kept her eyes trained strictly ahead, not only for safety but she refused to let her mind wander to that night when Lincoln's car breached one of those guardrails and plummeted into a ravine.

Far too often, she played the scene mentally at night while trying to capture sleep. She didn't need to go there now—didn't need to form those images and add them to her crowded mind.

As if knowing what she was thinking, Alani reached and patted her forearm.

Before long, the familiar Hana Bay and its black sand beaches came into view. The narrow roadway curved east, to the right for about a mile before they passed a broken-down school bus that had been parked for so long foliage and vines had covered the front bumper, not far from a welcome sign to the quiet town of Hana, long considered one of the last unspoiled Hawaiian frontiers.

Heading into the tiny town, they passed several buildings that looked to be out of another time—small, unassuming structures, some brightly colored. Retail signs were often hand-painted. A secondhand clothing store was located next to a dingy-looking gas station, and there was a live goat tethered outside an eatery.

Alani extended her neck out the open window for a better look. "What's the address?"

Ava slowed and grabbed her phone where she'd earlier plugged in the address. The property was located on Uakea Road not far from Kaueokahi Beach.

Minutes later, they pulled in front of a very small structure with a wraparound porch. Unlike some of the surrounding houses, the property was neat and well-landscaped with palms, monstera bushes, and poinsettia plants with pink and red blooms. A rock path cut through a lush green lawn and led to the front door.

"Well, here it is," Ava said, shutting off the engine. She stared, trying to take it in, trying to conjure yet again why Lincoln had purchased the property and not told her.

"It's cute," Alani said.

Ava took a deep breath. "Yeah, it is. Shall we go check it out?"

They climbed from the car and made their way to the porch. Ava used the key Christel had given her and opened the front door.

From the property records Ava had researched, the house was less than a thousand square feet, had only one bedroom and a tiny bath. No garage.

Inside, the living area was sparsely furnished. There was a rattan sofa and chair, a wooden coffee table stacked with magazines. The adjoining kitchen had painted green cabinets with hardware that was popular in the fifties. A very small table and two chairs were tucked against a wall covered in woven bamboo near a tiny refrigerator that stood not much taller than Ava. The house was clean and well-kept with what appeared to be handmade curtains on the small-paned windows.

"Wow," Alani said as she examined the interior. "It's small."

"It's not what I expected," Alani murmured. "I think we can rule out vacation rental."

Ava moved for the open-railed stairs. "The bedroom must be up here."

Together, they climbed the narrow stairway, which opened to a single room with a queen bed, neatly made with a handmade quilt draped over the end of the comforter. A pair of Lincoln's shoes were tucked near the bedside table. To the right, a door led to a tiny bathroom with a ceramic-tiled floor and a pink sink.

Ava mustered her courage and moved in that direction. Her mouth gaped open as she saw two toothbrushes in a glass on the counter.

Alani saw it too and grabbed her hand. "Oh, Ava. No."

Tears blurred Ava's vision as she turned back for the bedroom. No...no! This was all wrong. Lincoln? How could she not have known? How could she not have seen what was happening right beneath her nose? The queen-sized bed filled her vision, every aspect of it...the carefully tucked corners, the fluffed pillows. Ava's teeth clenched so hard she thought the back ones might break. Her eyes trailed up, up to a spot above the headboard.

Her heart stopped. A sudden intake of air pulled the oxygen from her lungs. Ava swayed.

Centered on the wall in a frame was a print engraved with the following words:

Ua ola loko I ke aloha.

The same phrase written on the piece of paper she'd found tucked in Lincoln's suit pocket on the day of the memorial service.

There was no escaping the possibility she'd dreaded most, the option she hadn't let herself dare mention out loud.

Lincoln had betrayed her.

Her hand immediately went to her neck. She couldn't breathe. "I—I need some air." She bolted for the stairs.

Alani looked at her with alarm. "Ava?"

Before chasing after her friend, Alani's gaze quickly darted to the framed print, her feet deadbolted to the floor as she tried to take in what she was looking at.

Her face immediately drained of color. "Oh, my sweet Lord Jesus!" she whispered.

11

Willa flipped through the TikTok images on her phone in silence as she sat at the back of the school bus. *This is so lame,* she thought, recalling the texts with her mother.

"Willa, please try and understand. I have a meeting with a potential construction manager for the bakery expansion. Your dad has two wedding parties tonight with two different custom menus," her mother had written.

Willa quickly texted back, reminding her that it was Friday night. No one else had to come straight home from school, let alone ride the school bus, better known as the wheels of shame.

"I'll make it up to you," her mother promised.

Willa clicked off the social media app and let her phone drop to her lap. Her mother's promises were piling up. She could no longer count the times her mother had lured her with bribes if she would only do this or that. How many hours had she babysat her little sister while her friends were surfing? How many loads of laundry? She was likely the only girl in her class who cooked herself meals at least twice a week.

Not one of her friends had to deal with this. Their moms were home and cooked dinner and stuff. Okay, sure...her own mom was pretty cool in a lot of ways, but she was single-handedly wrecking her social life.

Her phone buzzed, and she lifted it to find a text from her new friend. Amanda Cooper had moved to Maui last month from Houston.

"Hey, my mom said she'd drop me off at your house later. Want some company?" she wrote.

"Sure!" Willa quickly typed back, her thumbs working the letters furiously.

"Great. I really need to see you. TTYL."

Willa clicked off her phone, unable to suppress a grin. Her Friday night had been salvaged after all.

While Willa hadn't known Amanda long, she'd liked her instantly. She was cool and smart. You could instantly tell she was from Texas because of the way she talked, saying funny things like, "I'm fixin' to go get a soda. Y'all want one?"

Willa couldn't imagine moving into a new school and facing a bunch of strangers. Amanda didn't seem the least bit bothered. She walked into algebra class that first morning like she owned the place. Willa had never seen anyone so confident. And Amanda was cute...like someone off a television show.

The boys all sure liked her. A week hadn't even gone by, and Amanda had a date...a real date, the kind where the boy picked you up and paid. Every girl in school was jealous when Josh Adelmann asked her out.

Amanda Cooper never rode the school bus.

The school bus lumbered onto Naniloa Drive and lurched to a stop at her house. She scrambled from the vinyl-covered seat and made her way to the front. The door opened.

"Thanks," she said to the driver before clipping down the steps onto the pavement.

A thought occurred to her as she headed across the lawn.

On those occasions when her mom was tied up and couldn't pick her up from school—which seemed pretty frequent lately—maybe she'd be allowed to catch a ride home with Amanda. She was sure Mrs. Cooper wouldn't mind.

She dug out her key and unlocked the front door. Inside, she was immediately met by Givey. She bent and rubbed the dog's ears. "Hey, girl. Miss me?" She moved to the kitchen, grabbed a soda and a bag of chips, and headed straight for her room. If she got her history essay out of the way before Amanda arrived, they could study for the earth science test together.

It wasn't long before the doorbell rang.

Willa scrambled off the bed and took the stairs two at a time. She bolted to the door and flung it open. "Hey!" she said, greeting her friend.

Amanda brushed past her. "Are we alone?"

"Yeah. Why?"

Her friend walked directly into the kitchen. She tossed her bag onto the counter and dug inside. When she pulled her hand up, she held a small box.

"What's that?" Willa said, bending over with curiosity to get a better look. Suddenly, her eyes went wide. "A pregnancy test?"

"Shhh...yeah, a pregnancy test."

"Where'd you get that?" she asked, shocked.

"At the drugstore, silly." Amanda looked around. "Where's your bathroom?"

Willa nearly choked in surprise. "The test is for you?"

Amanda rolled her eyes. "Where's the bathroom?" she repeated, not bothering to hide her impatience.

Willa swallowed and pointed to the guest bath door. "In there. But, don't you have to take that test first thing in the morning?"

Amanda held the box up. "Nope. It's recommended but not

required." A look passed over her face that betrayed her air of confidence. "I'll be right back."

Willa grabbed for her arm. "Wait! Are you…I mean, are you scared?"

Amanda closed her eyes, swallowed. "Don't freak, okay? Just let me go take this test." She went into the bathroom, shut the door.

Minutes seemed like hours as Willa waited for that door to open again. She bent and stroked the fur on Givey's back while her mind raced with possibilities. Was Amanda pregnant? If so, that meant she'd been with Josh in *that* way. Willa knew there were lots of kids at school claiming to have gone there, but truthfully? She thought most of them were exaggerating. She'd been accused of being naïve. Perhaps she was.

A noise from outside pulled her attention. It was her mom! She was home.

Willa frantically glanced around before rushing to the bathroom door. She pounded. "Amanda, my mom's home. You have to hurry!"

Silence. The door remained closed.

Willa jiggled the doorknob. Locked. She pounded again. "Amanda! Did you hear me?" she shouted. "My mom! She's back."

The front door opened and in walked her mother carrying Noelle. Her toddler sister held a stuffed animal in her hand. "See my *dinotore*?" she asked. "Grrr…" she growled in her little girl voice.

Willa glanced over her shoulder, her heart pounding. "Hey," she said weakly.

"How was school, honey?" her mom asked as she set her sister on the floor. "I'm sorry I couldn't pick you up. You can't imagine how busy I am. First, the contractor manager was late by fifteen minutes. Then, he failed to bring the proper plans with him. He had the ones without my recent changes." She tossed her purse on the counter and moved for the refrigerator. "I have no idea what I'm going to cook for dinner." She straightened. "Hand me my phone, would you, honey? I'll call your dad and see what time he expects to be home. Likely late, with those dinner parties going on."

The guest bathroom door opened and out walked Amanda. "Hi, Mrs. Briscoe!"

"Oh...hello, Amanda. I forgot you were coming over." Without waiting for Willa to do so, she moved for her purse and retrieved her phone. "You girls up for some pizza?"

Willa turned to her friend, scowled.

In response, Amanda gave her a wide grin and shook her head, almost imperceptibly. Apparently, the test was negative.

Willa let out a breath she wasn't even aware she'd been holding. "Yeah, pizza." She glanced back at Amanda. "Do you like pepperoni?"

Amanda shrugged. "Who doesn't?"

12

Ava walked out of her house at the crack of dawn, holding her cup of coffee. Inside, her bed remained untouched. Throughout the night, she'd sat in Lincoln's favorite chair looking out over the lanai, watching the sky darken. The numbness lifted, and she felt every bit of it—the pain and the shame she would silently wrestle with every day of her life.

The images in that house kept replaying in her mind. The tiny ceramic pot on the counter next to the kitchen sink filled with succulents. While the plants didn't require daily watering, someone tended to them often enough to keep them alive. The stack of *Glamour* magazines on the coffee table. The lavender bathroom towels. Not a color her husband would choose.

The evidence was everywhere.

But it wasn't until she saw the framed quote on the wall above the bed that her mind finally caved and accepted what she'd tried desperately to deny.

Who was she...this woman? Her mind raced through a mental list of females who had attended Lincoln's funeral. One of them slipped that piece of paper in his suit pocket. But, who?

The church had a foyer that opened to the pristine gardens. Anyone could have had access to the church in the hours prior to the service. Security had been the last thing on her mind as she made preparations for her husband's memorial.

Ava hated the fact that this homewrecker had a few private seconds with him. Likely he'd been with her the night of the accident, which meant this woman was the last person to see her husband alive. The last hours of his life were spent with her. Not with his own wife, the woman who'd declared "for better or for worse" all those years ago—and had meant it. The woman who gave her life to him, raised children with him, sacrificed in order to build a successful business.

So, who walked boldly into the Chapel at Wailea with enough privacy to pull an action like that off? Why had no one noticed?

She fought to breathe as her thoughts trailed...

Had Lincoln been in love with her?

There it was. The question that plagued her the most as she'd gazed out at the blackness of night.

The drive home had been a blur. Neither Ava nor Alani had said more than ten words—which was out of character for Alani, even in this. Yet, what could either of them say?

Her worst fears had been realized. The discovery of Lincoln's betrayal created a deeper wound than even his death. She'd been lied to. Her marriage was a sham...and she hadn't even known.

She couldn't help but ask herself what she'd done...or hadn't done...to drive him into another woman's arms.

"Are you...okay?" Alani had finally asked, her voice barely above a whisper.

"I'm fine."

She made it clear it was far too early...she didn't want to discuss any of this. Not yet. Maybe not ever.

Thankfully, Alani didn't argue.

Lincoln's betrayal had sliced deep. Ava wasn't going to let others see her bleed...not even her best friend. She especially did not want the children to know. Lincoln was dead. What was the point of shattering their worlds now? Why allow them to wrestle with this knowledge? Wasn't it bad enough the foundation beneath her own feet had shifted? She'd never even known anything was wrong with their marriage, never imagined this possible.

Her myriad of questions would never be answered. She couldn't scream, "Who is she?" She couldn't demand to know when it started, how they met, what had so strongly attracted him to her that he would break his vow.

Bottom line? Lincoln wasn't even the man she thought she knew. She'd been grieving a person who didn't exist. The man she buried was a cheat, a self-centered person who believed his feelings mattered more than his wife and family's. He was one of *those*...the adulterers she so disrespected. Despised, actually.

This discovery forced her to suffer yet another death...that of her love for her husband. She would never again think of him fondly.

So, what now?

She'd gifted Lincoln with years of her life, given him four wonderful children. Pali Maui was hers. Upon marrying her, he'd been handed a successful business and never had to earn his way without depending on her...not really.

Yes, they'd worked to build the pineapple plantation together. Yet the day-to-day operations and decisions ultimately fell to her, especially since Lincoln traveled so often. Now she wondered...had he taken those trips alone?

Ava couldn't exactly recall the last time Lincoln romanced her, let her know he was feeling needy. She could remember their sex life dwindling, all but disappearing. The change was so gradual she couldn't put a time on it, but it had been a while. Even if she'd recognized the issue, she'd have brushed it off to the fact they both worked so hard. Neither of them could spare the sleep.

Besides, their lives had grown into so much more. They used each other for sounding boards about pricing, shipping and marketing decisions. When it came to family, they shored each other up, at least one of them always being there for the kids...both when they were young and now.

On the evenings they were both at home and could relax with a glass of wine, their time wasn't consumed in passion. It was companionship that filled the hours—conversation, laughter and advice for each other. Maybe a movie or quiet time while they both read. A perfect partnership. Or so she'd believed.

Didn't he owe it to her to say something? If he'd been forthcoming and revealed he was disappointed in their relationship, she'd have tried to fix it. Lincoln hadn't even given her that chance. He'd simply moved on and led a double life, had gotten his needs met elsewhere. What kind of mate does that? How could someone who had promised to cherish her forever treat her in such a shabby manner?

Lincoln had lied. He was a cheater. Had broken his promises. She would never forgive him. Yet, even that fortress failed to protect her crushed and splintered heart.

Ava quickly pushed the thought from her mind. He didn't deserve one more minute of her life going forward. No one had the power to destroy you unless you give them that ability.

Even as she thought these things, she knew it was impossible—naïve, even—to think moving past Lincoln's betrayal would be easy. She'd have to muster every ounce of mental strength...for her own sake and for her family.

Ava lifted the steaming mug of coffee to her lips as she

walked in the direction of the packing sheds. Her hands wanted to tremble. But like she said, she wasn't the sort to sink into an emotional mire at the hand of someone else...and she wasn't going to turn into that kind of person now.

13

Alani maneuvered her car into the tight space in the parking lot and shut off the engine. She grabbed her purse and exited the vehicle, then walked the lengthy pathway to the entrance of the Hyatt Regency. True to its marketing brochures, the forty-acre resort was located on Ka'anapali Beach and featured high-rise buildings with rooms overlooking the ocean. The hotel was a tourist favorite, and for good reason. The luxury resort offered every amenity, including multiple sparkling blue pools lined with cabanas, outstanding five-star restaurants, and even a daily penguin feeding.

"*Aloha*, Mrs. Kané," the concierge said in greeting as Alani made her way into the spacious atrium lobby with shiny tiled floors and potted tropical plants.

Breathless from the brisk walk, Alani waved back. "*Aloha!*" Often, she'd stop and chat. Not today.

With determination, she pointed to the area behind the registration desk. "Is Mia in?"

The concierge nodded. "Yeah. I saw her a few minutes ago. Do you want me to tell her you're here?"

"No, that's fine." Alani lifted her chin. She brushed past him and marched in the direction of her daughter's office.

Alani was totally devoted to her children. Her pregnancy had come later in life and after several miscarriages. Her pregnancy with the twins had been determined high risk, forcing her on bed rest for months prior to the birth. She'd have done that three times over and more. Nothing in her life gave her more joy than her children.

Raising Ori and Mia had been an honor she and Elta had firmly embraced. The twins were a gift from God, and they promised they would not falter in teaching them to live according to his holy word and their Hawaiian heritage. They were to be respectful, do the right thing—even if the cost was high. Alani taught by example how to love lavishly, even when the other person fell short of deserving that love.

The strict upbringing had reaped rewards. Alani was able to proudly claim both her children had grown into amazing and generous people she not only adored, but was extremely proud of. Which was why the task ahead tugged at her like a leash.

Mia glanced up from her desk, startled by Alani's surprise visit. "Mom? What are you doing here?" Her eyes drifted to her desk calendar as if checking to see if she forgot a scheduled lunch date.

"I need to talk with you." Alani had a sweet, heart-shaped face to go with her plump body. But the glare she gave her daughter was anything but pleasant.

Mia slowly lifted from her office chair as Alani turned to shut the office door. Her hands fidgeted with her long black hair, tucking one side behind her ear. Her face filled with worry, as if her mother had turned into a strange dog ready to bite. "I...I have a meeting in a few minutes."

Alani's eyes filled with tears. "Your meeting can wait."

Mia sunk back into her chair. She said nothing.

Alani could barely choke out her next words. "I know."

"Know?"

"About you and Lincoln."

The statement hung between them—heavy, painful, like little shards of glass, cutting and scraping until they met bone. Mia's eyes darted back and forth across the room as if seeking escape where there was none. Seconds ticked by before she allowed her gaze to meet her mother's. "I can explain."

That's all it took. Those three words were confirmation of the thing Alani most feared was true. She'd hoped for some strange kind of misunderstanding or even an explanation, a denial...something that would counter the veracity of the gut-wrenching accusation.

Alani's hand flew to her mouth as if to stop the bile that instantly roiled in her gut. Her Mia had done the unthinkable. Her precious daughter had not only betrayed everything she'd been raised to believe in, but Mia had crossed a sacred boundary with a man who was totally out of bounds. Lincoln was a married man. Ava's husband—her *best friend's* husband.

Their families had gone on vacation together, had holidays together. Ava kept Alani's children when they had the chickenpox so Alani could perform her duties at the luau. When Ava had no sewing skills to speak of, Alani helped out by making costumes for her children for the big community stage play. Their families were so entwined it was difficult to separate where the Briscoes started and the Kanés left off.

The pill of this truth was a bitter one to swallow.

Alani's next words were measured by immense pain. "When did this all start?"

Mia's response came quickly. "The details don't matter."

"Don't matter?" Alani's voice rose several octaves. "Oh, they matter! All of this matters." Tears cascaded down her cheeks. She leaned forward and pointed a finger at the young woman sitting across the desk...a girl she barely knew anymore. In less than twenty-four hours, her darling Mia had morphed into a stranger. The loss was unbearable.

"How could you do something so wrong? It is a sin! You have committed adultery with a married man. Your callous actions hurt people, Mia. Me...your father...your brother. More, do you have any idea what Ava is feeling? My best friend was grieving the loss of her husband, and now she is forced to suffer *this*? Your selfishness has sliced her in two like a bayonet! What a miserable act. Surely you—"

"Mom, wait. Please, let me explain." Mia came from around her desk. Her arms reached for her mother. When Alani stepped back, the rejection caused Mia to drop her head before quietly adding, "I loved him."

Alani's eyebrows shot up. "Loved him?"

Before Alani was able to form another thought, her hand lifted. She slapped her daughter's face. Hard.

The action caused Alani's breath to catch. It was as if her hand had become a foreign object with a mind of its own.

Mia's palm immediately lifted to the red spot on her cheek. Her eyes darkened. "Leave!" She pointed to the door. "It's time for you to go."

Alani drew her chest up with indignation. "Yes, I'll go." She nodded. "I'll leave filled with shame for my daughter." The words crushed her spirit as she spoke them. Despite her fury, she longed for nothing more than to reach for her daughter and embrace her...tell her everything was going to be all right.

But everything wasn't all right.

Alani slowly let out her breath and turned to go.

"Mom? Wait." Mia paused. "How did you know?"

Alani turned to face her. "You are a careless girl, Mia. In many ways." Alani stared at her daughter in defeat. "You hung Grand Ma-ma's print above the bed." Her heart ached as she added, "*Ua ola loko I ke aloha.* Love gives life within." She shook her drooping head. Her voice was measured and full of pain as she quietly added, "You have much to learn about this love, Mia."

Her ballooning grief imploded into an abyss of utter despair. Alani slowly pulled the door open. Fighting the temptation to look back, she walked away.

14

Jon pulled his favorite mug from the kitchen cupboard and finally poured himself a cup of coffee. Katie had made a pot before she left for the airport early in the morning for a quick overnight trip to Honolulu. She had a meeting with suppliers and promised to be home as early as possible. In the meantime, running Household Ackerman fell to him.

He moved to the hallway, steaming mug in hand. "Hurry up, Willa. You're going to be late."

"Willa late. Willa late," Noelle repeated, her pudgy toddler legs swinging from her high chair. Her fingers dove into the bowl of milk, and she fished out a final Cheerio and popped it in her mouth.

"Hey, you little goof," Jon chided as he lifted his tiny daughter from her chair. "Let's get you cleaned up, shall we?" Noelle kicked her feet with glee, spilling the bowl. Jon groaned as a stream of milk flowed over the list Katie had left for him. A list that held detailed instructions on how to dress the girls, what time they had to be dropped off at school and daycare, the items he'd need to pick up at Target for Willa's upcoming rally at school. Their daughter was in charge of decorations, an appointment she took seriously. "Don't forget," Katie had written and circled. Twice.

Jon held Noelle midair as he watched the ink on the list fade. "Sorry Da da," his little girl apologized. He ruffled her sweat-matted hair. "No worries, sweetheart. Accidents happen."

"Dad!" Willa called from down the hall. "I can't find my blue socks."

Jon put Noelle down and grinned, wondering just what he was supposed to do about the missing socks.

"Never mind! Found them."

Unlike many fathers, Jon relished the happy chaos of their home—a chaos Katie attempted to manage. Sometimes successfully.

Minutes later, Willa appeared in the kitchen. Jon was standing at the sink, rinsing the dishes before placing them in the dishwasher. "Dad! We're going to be late," she warned.

"Okay, okay. Get Noelle and let's head out." He turned to find Willa scowling. "What?"

"Is that what Noelle is wearing today? I doubt very much that's the outfit Mom chose."

"Look," Jon said, waving her off. "Be a sweetheart and go change your sister. I'll go brush my teeth, and we'll get going. I'll get you to school on time. Promise."

He wasn't so sure he could keep the promise, but he was a cup-half-full kind of guy. In the spirit of that optimism, he quickly headed for the guest bath, where he kept a spare toothbrush. He'd learned a few things living with a household of women...not the least of which was that he was often the last one to have a turn in the other bathrooms.

He pulled the drawer open and retrieved his toothbrush and a half-empty tube of toothpaste. He'd forgotten to put the lid back on last time he'd used it, and the opening was clogged. Jon used his thumb to flick the old toothpaste off, creating a projectile that landed on the floor. He knew better than to leave it there. Katie would have a fit if she stepped on it.

He leaned to pick it up, and that's when he saw a little blue tube peeking out from under a wad of toilet paper in the waste can. The shape was familiar.

His breath grew shallow as he pulled the implement from the trash and slowly held it up for inspection.

Positive.

Jon's sight momentarily blurred. Then his face broke into a big, wide grin.

His Katie was pregnant again!

KATIE RAN down the concourse dragging a wheeled briefcase behind her. She didn't often wear heeled pumps, but this was an important business meeting and she needed to make an impression.

She hit the gate with a hand lifted high. "Wait! I'm here." Minutes earlier, a last-call announcement had broadcast over the intercom causing her heart to pound. She was never late. In fact, she made a point of being at least ten minutes early for every appointment. This morning, she'd run into a clog of traffic. While she loved the thriving tourist trade here on Maui and made a lot of money serving island visitors, she still despised the added cars on the roadways.

The gate attendant gave her a wide smile. "Go on. You're fine." The woman leaned forward and winked. "We always give that announcement a little early," she admitted. "For the habitually late travelers."

Katie returned the smile and handed her phone over so the woman could scan the barcode on her digital ticket.

"There you go." The gate attendant waved her on.

Katie thanked her and moved down the jet bridge. She

greeted the flight attendant at the door of the plane and quickly found her seat. She stowed her briefcase, and slipped into the tiny spot and buckled herself in. After checking her watch, she pulled out her phone and hit the speed dial number for her sister.

Christel picked up on the first ring. "Hey, sis. What's up?"

Katie explained about her necessary trip. "I wasn't able to talk to Mom this morning. Could you check on her? She's been acting funny lately."

"Funny?"

"Yeah. She's been very quiet since that day with Alani. I'd hoped the time away would do her good. Mom went right back to working herself around the clock. Mig tells me he has seen her house lights on in the middle of the night. She's up and going over production reports before dawn and rarely heads for the house until well after dark."

"Well, that's just Mom," Christel argued.

Katie shifted in her seat and glanced out the tiny porthole. "Yes, but I don't think she's sleeping. And, she looks like she's losing weight again. Her clothes are hanging off her, Christel. I leave food in her fridge, and even her favorite dishes often remain untouched. Just yesterday, I tried to get her to come look at the paint colors for the bakery addition, and she declined. I mean, I know she's busy, but she always makes time when you ask her for something."

"Give her a break, Katie. She's still grieving."

"Yes, I know that but...well, she just seems different." Katie leaned back to allow her seatmate to move into his spot. He looked to be in his forties and wore an expensive suit. They exchanged polite smiles.

"Okay, I'll make a point of inviting her for dinner, if she'll go. I'll see what I can find out."

"Thanks," Katie said. "And will you do me another favor?"

She could almost hear her sister sigh over the phone.

"Check on Shane, too. Now that Dad's gone, we all need to step up. Mom spoils him, and Dad was the only one who seemed to keep him in line."

"Katie, he's an adult. He can take care of himself."

"He's twenty-three. Technically, an adult. But we both know the term is defined loosely when it comes to our little brother." Katie paused. "If you talk to Aiden, tell him the same. It takes a village and all that." Katie knew her sister was a Hillary Clinton fan. She wasn't above using any tool necessary to sway her sister into her line of thinking, including a phrase her idol had made famous.

"Okay, okay...look, I've got to go. Quarterlies are due tomorrow, and I've got hours of work ahead of me. Safe travels."

"All right. Bye, sis." Katie clicked off her phone. She smiled at the man in the suit. "Sorry, my sister." She tucked her cell phone back in her purse.

He smiled. "No problem."

Katie leaned back as the stewardess started her safety spiel over the intercom. In her world, there were two kinds of men—suits and flannels. She adored her flannel, appreciated the way he could fix things, was a master in culinary arts, and could juggle family and work without breaking a sweat.

While she loved her man and could never betray him—not in a million years—she had to admit she had great appreciation for nice suits.

15

Shane climbed from his topless Jeep and reached for his backpack. He threw it over his shoulder and headed through the parking garage and through the grounds of the Sheraton. On the path he passed a family heading out to Ka'anapali Beach. The father towed a cooler on wheels while the mother struggled to hang onto the hand of a toddler. Two young boys raced ahead on the path until the father warned them not to get too far ahead.

Shane smiled. The scene could've been a flashback to when he was young. Ka'anapali Beach was a favorite destination for the Briscoes and they came here often, together with the Kanés. Much later, he'd realized nearby restrooms and plenty of eating establishments along the strip of resort hotels had been a factor playing into choosing this beach. As he and his siblings grew older, the family migrated to other beaches that were not so packed with tourists.

One of his buddies who worked at the Sheraton as a pool attendant waved. "Hey, dude! I should be off in forty minutes and can join you guys."

Shane nodded and gave him the famous pinky and thumb

salute. "Shaka, brah!" The large lava rock cropping known as Black Rock loomed ahead. Already, the crest was filled with jumpers. It was a perfect morning for a few rock dives. Sunny, clear, and little wind.

When he reached the pinnacle, he exchanged fist bumps with some of the locals, guys he'd grown up with. They were barefoot and wore board shorts. Some had long hair, and nearly all of them sported a tat of some sort on their darkly tanned shoulders.

A nearby sign read: *No Diving. Do not go beyond this point. Serious injury or death possible.* Shane shrugged off the warning just as he had numerous times, knowing the legal department had a hand in protecting the city or state from liability. While true, injuries had occurred when cliff diving—the incidents were rare and often the product of tourists being stupid. None of the locals would risk jumping when it was really windy or when dangerous currents moved in.

Of course, his mother would argue wildly that was not true. Christel would also throw her two cents in reminding him that the business health insurance policy had exceptions. Reckless behaviors topped the list. His dad? Well, his dad would have just given him "the look." The list of things his father disapproved of was long. His list of disappointing behaviors could compete.

"Son, in life, you have to dive deeper than the shallow end," he'd often told Shane. "You're capable of so much more than the effort you're putting in."

Despite always falling short in his dad's eyes, it wasn't until he was gone that Shane recognized the worth of a good father. He had been lucky to have one who loved him in the womb long before he even officially arrived on the scene. A dad who would come looking for him when he couldn't find his way home. One who was missed so terribly, everything fell apart in his absence.

One of the divers ran his hand through the top of his long hair. "This spot is dope."

Shane grinned at him and tossed his backpack on top of the sharp, craggy lava rocks. "So, yeah. Let's get a little reckless!"

Another kid behind him who didn't look old enough to be out of high school chimed in, "Don't land on any turtles."

Shane gazed out over the water that was at least a dozen shades of blue—azure, cobalt, teal, and turquoise all mixed together. The water was clear, and from up here, he could spot rocks and white sand below the surface.

In the distance, kayakers slowly made their way across the incoming waves. The beach was filled with bright-colored umbrellas and beach chairs. Chicks with suits that barely covered the essentials rubbed oil on long, tan legs. The sight made his breath catch a little.

"You're up, dude," one of the guys said, pounding him on the back with an open palm. "Go for it."

Another said, "Hey, nobody die today!"

Shane took a step back feeling the sharp lava cut into the sole of his foot. He fought the urge to let an expletive rip when he saw her—the perky blonde waitress from Charley's. Her mouth drew into a slow smile. "Hey," she said.

"Hey," Shane answered. "Great to see you again."

"Dude! You going?" one of the guys shouted at him. "'Cause this girl is way out of your league—"

Shane stepped back, bent, and grabbed his towel from off his backpack and wrapped it around his neck. "Yeah, you go ahead. I'll take my chances here." He winked at her.

Her face broke into a wide smile. Long blonde hair cascaded over one shoulder. Her bikini revealed deep cleavage. Nice. Her tan skin shimmered, body toned in all the right places. She had a tattoo on her upper arm—a long-stemmed rose. She was hot…and she was making him hot. And he wasn't talking sunshine here.

"Aimee, wasn't it? From Chicago?"

"You remembered," she confirmed. "And, if I remember correctly, you were going to call me." She threw him a mock glare, her body language conveying her interest.

He ran his hand through his hair. "Yeah...yeah, about that. I'm not good with numbers. Seems I misplaced that little paper you wrote on." He gave her an exaggerated shrug.

Her lips went into a pout. "You lost my number? That's not a good sign."

"Oh, but—" His hand went to his chest like he was having a heart attack. "The pain was unbearable when I realized I had no way to contact you."

Her eyes narrowed, and she bit her bottom lip. "You could have just come back into the restaurant."

He took a step closer. "No. I was far too distraught."

That made her giggle. "Well, I guess we'll have to fix this, won't we?"

Before he could answer, she ran for the edge and leapt off.

It took a second for it to sink in. As many times as he'd dove off Black Rock, his heart still pounded a little before jumping. She'd exhibited no fear.

Without another thought, he followed, suddenly so clumsy he felt like Bambi learning to walk. He tossed his towel on the ground as he ran to the edge and leapt. He became airborne, freefalling a couple of seconds before he tucked and held his knees in a spin. He released just before entering the surface.

White clouded his vision as bubbles tickled his torso. He went deep, opened his eyes to see her several feet away swimming for the surface. A sea turtle drifted slowly in the distance.

Seconds later, he broke the surface and gasped for air. He quickly looked around and spotted her head only a few feet from him. "That was *kamaha'o*!" he shouted.

. . .

SHE GRINNED BACK AT HIM, and when she did, deep dimples appeared at the sides of her mouth.

His mother had trained him never to use an animal name to describe a girl. Even so, this chick was a fox—a smoking hot fox with long blonde hair and longer legs. A girl he wouldn't mind following back to her den.

AIDEN PICKED up on the first ring. "Hey, Shane. What's up?"

"Bro! Remember that girl in the restaurant?"

Shane dipped his brush in the can of paint and held it midair. "The restaurant?"

"Yeah. That blonde from Charley's. The one who gave me her number. Well, I hooked up with her today. She was up at Black Rock. Dude, you should see that girl dive. No fear. None."

Aiden placed his brush on the wall of his bathroom and swept it downward in a long stroke. "Yeah?"

"She's amazing! Like we swam for a while, and then we went into Lahaina and we ate at Star Noodle. She talked me into trying these little steamed pork buns. We discovered we both love udon noodles, but only in beef broth without any meat. With extra sesame oil. She's...well, I think I'm in love."

Aiden knew his little brother was exaggerating. "True love, huh?"

"Oh, yes," Shane assured him. "*Absolute*, commit for a *lifetime* love."

"Or at least until the next morning?"

"Yeah, that too," Shane admitted.

"So, what's next?" Aiden dipped his brush back in the can.

"Next? Yeah, well...I'm picking her up tomorrow and we're going to kayak. She's from Chicago and they kayak some lake there."

"Lake Michigan."

"What? No, she's in Illinois," his little brother corrected.

"Dude. Lake Michigan borders Illinois. That's the lake in Chicago she was referring to." Aiden rolled his eyes. He stepped back and inspected his work. Katie had helped him choose between metal gray and mushroom gray. The mushroom color was spot on. "So, you're going to see her again. That's great, bro." Aiden chuckled, wondering what had happened to his little brother...the guy who would never openly admit he had feelings for a girl.

"Yeah. Hey, you talked to Mom lately? 'Cause she's usually riding my case pretty hard, and I haven't heard from her in days. I tried to call and she didn't pick up. I even left messages."

"I think we're all going to have to go light on Mom, Shane. She tries to hide it, but she's definitely still hurting." He wiped his paintbrush off with a cloth and set it across the can. He straightened and rubbed at the small of his back. His job required lots of physical effort, but nothing made his back ache like painting. "Look, sounds like it might be time for all of us to show up for dinner. I'll see if Jon can cook up something special. Sound like a plan?"

"Yeah, that'd be good."

"And, Shane?" Aiden paused.

"Yeah?"

"Wanna bring the girl?"

"Nah, I said I was in love. I didn't say I wanted to marry her."

Aiden laughed. There was the little brother he knew.

16

"Alani, sweetheart. What is it?" Elta drew his sobbing wife into his arms and pressed her tightly against him. Alani was the strongest, most grounded woman he knew. Unlike some of their congregants, she never gossiped, rarely complained about life's difficulties, and often carried a smile on that sweet face of hers. Seeing her fall apart like this was a rarity. In fact, he wasn't sure he'd ever seen her this crushed in spirit.

Through sniffles, she pushed out a broken answer. "She-she...our Mia. Oh, Elta. Our Mia has done something terrible."

Elta extended his arm and closed the church office door. "Is she all right? Has she been in an accident?" He led his wife to the sofa, and they both sat.

Alani shook her head miserably. "No, nothing like that." She pulled back and looked at him with tears streaming. "We grounded her. Taught her right from wrong. Trained her to love God and follow him. And now she's—" His wife could no longer push out coherent words for the new outpour of sobs.

Elta brushed damp hair from his wife's forehead. "Alani, honey. Tell me what's going on." His heart pounded, both wanting and not wanting to understand what had his wife so upset. It must be awful.

Alani gazed at him through pain-filled eyes. "Our daughter is having an affair, Elta. With a married man. Or, I should say, she *had* an affair."

Elta's eyebrows shot up. His hand flew to his chest. "Are you sure?"

His wife quickly nodded. "Yes. I confronted her a little while ago and she failed to deny it. Actually, she confirmed the transgression, not in so many words. But the situation is clear."

"You say she had an affair? It is over now?"

Again, Alani nodded. "Oh, yes. But not by choice."

Elta rubbed his chin. "He ended it and went back to his wife?"

Alani chewed on her bottom lip, clearly not wanting to fully reveal this awful thing she knew.

"Honey, tell me. All of it," Elta urged.

His wife nervously picked at her bright turquoise floral muumuu. "Mia had an affair...with Lincoln Briscoe."

Elta didn't say anything. He couldn't. An affair with Lincoln? Impossible!

"I'm sure you misunderstood," he told Alani. "Our daughter would never—I mean, Lincoln would never..." Yet, as he looked at the pulverized emotions painted across his wife's face, he knew she was not kidding.

Elta sunk against the sofa cushions, barely able to draw a breath. Lincoln Briscoe was his friend. They'd known each other for years, had practically raised their families together. Lincoln had pushed a young Mia on the swings at the city park, had helped cut up her meat and had chased her around a makeshift soccer field as he and Elta taught the kids to dribble and block, and make the perfect head-shot.

The news gutted Elta.

He felt sick and unable to respond. All he could do was look at his beloved Alani with a shared disbelief and guilt. How had something so heinous happened between two people they so loved.

Anger quickly set in. Lincoln knew better!

He pounded his fist against the sofa. "Good thing he's dead, or I'd kill him!"

Alani quickly covered his fist with the palm of her hand. "Oh no, Elta. You mustn't say that."

Elta's eyes filled with tears. "I am a man of God. I am supposed to forgive. But this?" He shook his head in defeat. "This is unforgivable."

Suddenly, a thought hit him. "Where is she? Where's our Mia?"

"I went to her work and confronted her. When I angrily walked out, she remained behind."

Elta glanced about the room frantically. He stood and paced. "I—I'd better stay away for now. I don't know what to say to her." He looked at his wife, hopeful. "Tell me she's sorry. Does she understand the wrong she committed?"

"Oh, yes. She knows the affair was wrong, but she says she loved him," Alani explained. She went on to tell him about her unplanned trip to Hana with Ava and the reason for the trek. She told him all about the discovery of the house by the estate attorney and how Ava came to understand her husband had been keeping secrets—and ultimately, that he'd been having an affair. "Lincoln's things were there. In that house. His clothes and shoes. Personal items in the bathroom. And there were indications he had not been alone in this house." His wife then disclosed how she discovered the framed quote on the wall above the bed and recognized it as the same one Mia's grandmother had given to her before her passing. "Elta, Mia placed Grand Ma-ma's gift above her bed of sin."

Alani swallowed against that truth and continued. She told

him about the note Ava discovered in Lincoln's suit pocket before the funeral.

Elta felt nauseous. It hadn't yet sunk in how Ava played in all of this, how their daughter's affair had impacted her. Their dear friend was still in mourning, for goodness sakes. "How is Ava? What did she say?"

Alani plummeted her face into her hands and started crying again. "She doesn't know."

"Doesn't know?"

Alani lifted her face and looked at him, wrecked. "She doesn't know the woman was our Mia. I didn't tell her. I couldn't."

"Oh, my dear *wahine*. You cannot keep this from her." He gently took his wife's hand. "We must tell her." This new revelation weighed him down, the burden of it all too heavy. He looked up, hoping to find strength in the heavens. "This is the way of sin. It creates a tsunami of waves, capsizing everyone and everything it touches. That is why we are told to stay away from evil, to guard our hearts against its power."

His heart ached as he gazed at the photos on his wall, a parade of images capturing the twins as babies in Alani's arms, as toddlers running down the aisles of the church, shots of them graduating high school and then college. He'd hoped to soon see photos of them marrying and holding their own children in their arms.

What was he supposed to do with this knowledge?

Elta looked away. "Our girl thinks she loved him? That is not love. She was led astray and gave in to wrong." A single tear made its way down Elta's cheek. He brushed it away as he quietly quoted a proverb he'd long ago memorized. "Do not gaze at wine when it is red, when it sparkles in the cup, when it goes down smoothly. In the end it bites like a snake and poisons like a viper."

Those were the words that came from his mouth, but

another verse tugged at his heart. The one about training up a child in the way he should go. He had done his best as a pastor and as a father to properly educate his precious Mia, had tried to teach her right from wrong. Worse than the shame was the guilt.

Clearly, he had failed her.

17

Katie passed through the office lobby with its glossy tiled floors and tastefully decorated waiting area. To the left of the receptionist counter, a wide corridor led to a bank of office doors.

She approached the receptionist. "Hello, I'm Katie Ackerman. I'm here for a meeting with—" She paused, swallowed. "I'm here to see Greer Latham."

"Yes, his one o'clock," the woman said and pointed down the hall without looking away from her computer screen. "First set of double doors on the right. They're waiting for you."

Katie's breath caught. She snuck a glance at the clock on the wall behind the receptionist desk. She wasn't late. And *they*? She was led to believe the meeting was with Mr. Latham only. She swallowed. "Thank you."

She adjusted her briefcase strap on her shoulder and briskly headed toward the door the receptionist had pointed out. As her hand reached for the brass handle, a set of masculine fingers covered her own.

"Allow me."

Katie's gaze lingered on the bit of hair on the knuckles before glancing up.

The man's face drew into a slow smile—the man from the plane. Her seatmate. "It seems we've met," he said. "Well, in a manner of speaking."

After a tentative nod, she pulled her hand away and took a step back. "Yes, on the plane. I didn't know—"

She noted his thick, sandy-colored hair, cut to precision—that charcoal tailored suit and a crisp white button-down with a striped tie in shades of gray. His eyes never left hers as he eased the door open.

"Neither did I. I'm Greer Latham, and I assume you must be Ms. Ackerman?" She nodded and his face broke into a smile as he waved her inside. "Shall we?"

Katie followed him into a massive conference room, a showplace with ceiling-to-floor windows overlooking Waikiki Beach. The furnishings were old-world style, with dark woods and intricate molding. The plush carpet was a leaf design in shades of teal and cream.

A woman sat at the end of the table waiting with her fingers steepled. She had short-cropped silver hair and wore a white jacket trimmed in navy piping. She pushed her chair back and stood. "We're so glad our schedules allowed for this meeting, Ms. Ackerman." The woman extended her hand. "I'm Sylvia Latham...Chairman of Latham Enterprises."

A slight smile broke at the corners of Greer's mouth. "And my mother."

Katie shook her hand. "So nice to meet you." Mrs. Latham waved them over to a spot at the end of the long granite conference table.

Katie took her seat opposite Greer and busied herself unloading her briefcase with the documentation she'd spent the entire night before preparing. She set the stack in front of her and squared the edges so that the pile was neat and tidy.

Greer pulled at his right cuff. "The deal that's on the table is a bit tricky, but after reviewing the proposal, it is likely one we could make work." A smug assurance played across his face. "We certainly have the manufacturing capacity necessary to custom brand merchandise for your retail operation at the level you hope for."

"I agree," Mrs. Latham added. "You did an excellent job putting together the proposal and making the initial pitch."

Over the next hours, they meticulously reviewed all the deal points, the warehousing needs, the delivery expectations, the profit margins. Katie presented the additional documentation, arguing every attribute of the partnership she hoped they would form. While nervous, Katie focused on the details she'd meticulously memorized, pitching her ideas and negotiating for the best deal possible.

At the end of their time together, Mrs. Latham pushed her chair back from the table. "Well, dear. I'm in. This is an excellent opportunity for both of us. With our manufacturing capabilities and your retail venue and distinct marketing approach, I believe this deal has the potential to make both our companies a considerable profit." She paused. "And if necessary, we have a venture capital arm that we can access if additional funding is needed."

Katie beamed. She had to refrain from doing a fist pump. Christel had argued to attend this meeting but her sister wasn't the only one in the family who was capable of pulling off a profitable business coup with a prestigious firm. She couldn't wait to get to the airport to call and report her success. She may even gloat a little. She'd earned the right.

Her sister hadn't been entirely behind this project, making it clear taking on something of this magnitude might not be the best timing. Not on the heels of losing their father and all that entailed. Katie stood firm and had vehemently argued. "Timing is everything. An opportunity like this can't wait."

Christel eventually gave in, but not without warning how these projects often required far more work than originally expected.

Well, if that turned out to be the case, she'd deal with it.

Mrs. Latham stood. "You can work out the contract details with Greer."

Greer walked her out, and when they reached the reception area, he turned to her. "I'd like to drive you to the airport."

"That's a gracious offer, but I'm fine grabbing a cab."

"No, I insist," he said. "Tonya, I'll be out this afternoon."

The woman looked up from her computer monitor. "You have a four o'clock."

"Reschedule," he told her. "I won't be back." He placed his hand on the small of Katie's back. "Shall we?"

Minutes later, they were sitting in the plush backseat of a town car heading toward the airport, which was about thirty minutes away in good traffic. Still on a high after the business meeting, Katie used the opportunity to discuss the next step. "My sister is our corporate attorney. She'll be working with us to finalize the terms of the contract."

Greer's face immediately filled with disappointment. "Oh? I was hoping you and I would be working together to drill down on how to paper the deal—preferably over a pitcher of gin and tonics," he teased. "I promise, I'm a softy. You'll get away with plenty."

He pulled at his cuff again while telling her he'd formed Latham Enterprises after moving to Honolulu from San Antonio. "I was an executive at a bottled water company. Sadly, Mother faced a situation where she had to fire her entire board. She needed me here, and few people can say no to my mother." He grinned at her. "And I mean that with the utmost respect. She's highly capable."

"We have that in common. My own mother is a force to be reckoned with. We call her the *velvet hammer*." Katie gave him a quick rundown on Pali Maui—how her mom had inherited the pineapple plantation and, together with her father, had built the operation into a multi-million-dollar enterprise. They expanded crops, built a farm-to-market restaurant, a retail operation, and provided daily tours. "All of us siblings have worked at Pali Maui in some capacity. My brothers aren't currently serving in an official employment role, but they are still very much involved. We're a family-run organization."

Greer nodded. "You mentioned your father. I didn't see his name in the proposal."

Katie's throat closed a little. She coughed. "I'm afraid my father passed away recently. In an accident. Christel is in the process of amending our corporate documents. That effort will be completed before we ink this deal," she assured.

Greer's voice turned measured. "I'm so sorry to hear about your loss." He paused for several seconds. "If it's any consolation, you are the ultimate professional. No one would know you had just suffered losing your father."

She thanked him for the compliment. He inched closer so their knees were touching. "This might be off-topic, but I actually looked you up on the internet."

"On the internet?"

"Yes, and highly respected business sources assert you are the one with the vision in your family. I read a business article that claims it was you who realized the potential for tapping into the tourism aspect. The article went on to say the move was very profitable."

His compliment was unexpected. Rarely had Katie felt acknowledged and recognized for her contributions. "Thank you," she said. She smiled like a fool, overcome by the unexpected delight of having someone in the business world think so highly of her. A state she wasn't used to. "I'm often accused of racing ahead of what is prudent, but I do have a lot of ideas… good ones, I think."

"No doubt," he offered. "I think that is an essential quality for anyone who wants to race ahead of the pack. Integrated retail is a crowded venue, and those individuals willing to think outside of the box are twenty steps ahead."

Suddenly, a privacy panel lifted from the seat in front, separating them from the driver.

Katie glanced across at her seatmate, now nervous for a different reason. Her inner alert system woke up. Was he making a move on her?

This was not reassuring. She attempted to mask her discomfiture with a timid smile. "I...uh, let's go over warehouse needs again," she said, fumbling for her briefcase.

Greer leaned in, brashly placed his hand on her arm. "This business can be lonely for types like us. We're often misunderstood."

His intentions suddenly clarified and became very apparent. She scowled. "I'm afraid you're the one who misunderstood. I am not lonely, nor am I available." She flashed her wedding ring.

Greer shrugged. "That doesn't have to stand in the way."

Katie leaned back, appalled. "Are you kidding me? You're not really propositioning me in the backseat of a car? This is why you wanted to drive me to the airport?" She huffed.

His hand slipped to her cheek. "No one has to know."

She gave him a shove. "I don't think so."

He looked surprised. "I'm not sure I understand...or that you fully comprehend the complexity of the offer. Or, the consequences of turning me down."

Katie's eyes narrowed. She leaned forward and drilled him with a look that meant business, and not the monkey business he was proposing. "I am in no way interested in a #MeToo situation. I decline your offer, both this—" she knocked his hand off her knee, "—and the offer to partner with Latham. I'm done. Pali Maui is out of the deal."

His eyebrows raised. "You can't pull out now." He gripped her hand so forcefully that she felt one metacarpal bone crunch against another.

"Oh, yeah? Watch me!" She ripped her hand from his and banged on the partition. It lowered, and she told the driver to pull over and let her out.

"What are you doing?" Greer asked. "We're not yet at the airport."

"I'll walk," she said, grabbing her briefcase. "And you, sir. You are a puke."

The car came to a quick stop, and she pushed the passenger door open and scrambled out. "A real barf bucket." She slammed the door and marched away, dragging her overloaded briefcase behind.

Thankfully, she was able to flag down a cab and make her flight on time. While in the air, she rehearsed every moment of her conversations with Greer Latham, both by email and in person. What had she missed? Surely, there must've been signs. The fact she'd nearly climbed in a partnership with someone like that caused her to shudder. She would never do business with a predator. Not in a million years.

Unfortunately, the turn in the situation put her business idea back at square one. She'd have no option but to start over. There were other manufacturing operations out there. She'd simply have to do her research and approach another company. This was a setback, that was all.

A setback she would have to reluctantly explain to her sister.

Katie was still shaking when she deboarded the plane and made her way out to the pick-up area at the Kahului Airport on Maui. As promised, Jon was waiting for her.

"Where are the girls?" she asked when he rushed to her side.

"I left Willa with her little sister. She's cooking dinner." He pulled her briefcase into his hands. "Here, let me carry your bag." He opened the car door. "So, how are you feeling? Tired?"

Katie climbed in. "I'm fine. Why?"

Jon pulled the driver's side door open and got in. He put the car in gear and eased the vehicle into the slow-moving traffic. He handed her a wrapped sandwich. "Grilled portabella and Havarti. Thought you might be hungry. I know how you get when your stomach is empty." He looked at her with expectation.

She shook off his odd behavior. "Thanks," she said, taking the sandwich. "I didn't get a chance for lunch."

"That's not good for you," he reminded. "Especially in... well, in your condition."

Katie's face pulled into a puzzled frown. "Jon, what the Pete are you knocking around here? What do you mean by *condition*?" She reached in her purse for a tissue and wiped a spot on the dash.

He slowly grinned. "I know."

She directed her attention across the seat at her husband. "You know what?" she asked, unwrapping her sandwich.

He glanced in the side mirror and merged into the next lane. "I found the test in the bathroom. I know."

She paused her effort to unwrap the sandwich and gave him another look. "What test?"

In response, her husband reached and rubbed her belly. "In case you worried about it, I am thrilled. You could've told me straight up. We're in this together. You and me." He gunned the engine, speeding up. "The girls might need a minute to adjust, especially Willa. But me? I'm good." As if to punctuate his proclamation, he gave her a wide grin.

Katie let the sandwich drop to her lap. "What are you talking about?"

"You're pregnant."

"I'm what?" she asked, stunned.

His thumb patiently drummed the steering wheel. "We're having another baby."

She looked at him like he'd gone crazy. "I don't know what stove fumes you've been sniffing while I was gone, but we are *not* having another baby. What gave you that idea?"

"The test." Jon explained how he'd gone into the downstairs bath to brush his teeth, how he'd discovered a pregnancy test wrapped in tissue. A positive test.

"Well, I'm sorry, but that isn't my test. I'm not pregnant."

An alternate possibility dawned on them both at the same moment. Fear surfaced in their exchanged glances.

Breath left Katie's lungs as she forced a single whispered word through dry lips. "Willa."

18

Shane pulled back the sheets and sat up. Glancing over his shoulder, he had to take a minute to recall exactly how the sleeping blonde got there. Shots of coconut rum had been involved; he knew that.

He rubbed at his aching forehead.

Aimee...yes, that was her name. The waitress from Charley's. The girl at Black Rock with the knock-out body and sweet smile. They'd hooked up again. One thing led to another, and well...things happened. Good things.

His phone buzzed, and he withdrew it from the bed table, squinting to make out the tiny message displayed.

"Family meeting. Be over at Mom's in an hour."

Christel could even be bossy in her texts. He sighed and lifted from the bed, wondering if he had time for a shower before marching to his sister's orders. Maybe a quick one.

He checked on Aimee again. Sound asleep.

He quietly opened the Tylenol bottle and pushed two tablets down his throat, followed by some serious rehydration before heading to the bathroom. The morning after was not nearly as fun.

Shane turned on the shower faucet and waited for the water stream to turn steamy while he quickly brushed his teeth. He was in and out in less than five minutes, a new record.

Tucking his towel around his waist, he headed for the nearly empty closet, marveling at those who had time to do laundry—not something he personally made a priority. He bent and rummaged through the pile on the floor and produced his best-looking pair of jeans—albeit a bit wrinkled, and a favorite T-shirt which he pulled over his head.

Ah...he smelled coffee.

"Hey," he said as he headed in the direction of the aroma. "You're awake."

"I am," Aimee said, giving him a wide smile.

Shane pointed to the brewing coffee pot. "You didn't have to do that."

"I needed my caffeine fix." She held up her phone. "Looked and Starbucks was a little too far. Where exactly are we, anyway?" Despite their long night, this girl looked like a million bucks, especially when she smiled.

He reached for two mugs out of his cupboard, filled them, and handed one off to her. "Pali Maui. The pineapple plantation. I live here."

Aimee took the mug and drew the steaming cup to her lips, then walked over and peered out the window. "What's that over there?"

He looked over her shoulder. "That's my mom's house. The processing and packing sheds are there." He extended his finger in that direction. "And the restaurant and retail store over there. The offices are tucked back in that stand of palm trees. I can give you a tour sometime, if you want," he offered.

"Not the tour bus tour. A private tour." He nuzzled against her hair.

"Mmm...I'd like that. I had a great time last night. Got a little toasted, but I hope we can do it again sometime?"

Shane's heart skipped a beat. "Yeah...yeah, sure. I'd love that."

She leaned in and ran a finger down his stubbled cheek. "You're cute. You know that?"

He seized the opportunity and pulled her close, taking care not to spill their coffee. "You're not bad yourself." He kissed her. She tasted sweet, like spearmint gum mixed with a mocha flavor. And he recalled those lips from last night, soft and...

Man, he'd better stop now, or he'd never make it to his mom's house on time. As the past had shown, skipping out on a mandated family meeting had consequences. He couldn't afford rent on the island, not with his limited income. Given that, he'd play by the rules.

"Well, hey...I've got someplace I've got to be in a few," he told her. "Family obligations. But I really do want to see you again."

She flipped her long blonde hair off her shoulder and grinned. "How about tonight? My place?"

He walked her out, opened her car door and watched her climb in. "You bet! I'll call you later, and we'll confirm plans." She smiled and raised her eyebrows like she didn't totally believe him. "No, really. I'll call."

Aimee grabbed his phone and bumped the backside with hers, quick sharing their contact info. "There. No excuse. If you fail to keep your promise, I have your number," she reminded. "And, I'm not afraid to use it."

Shane leaned inside the open car window and brushed a kiss against Aimee's cheek. "Later," he said as she started the engine.

"Yup, later." She eased her car in reverse, turned, and slowly headed down the lane. He waved, and she stuck a hand out the open window and waved back.

Minutes later, Aiden's truck lumbered into the driveway

followed by Katie's SUV. Shane jogged over to meet them. "So, anyone know what this sudden meeting is all about?"

Aiden shook his head. "Nope. Christel just said to be there."

"And Christel loves to keep all the details to herself," Katie noted.

Shane and his siblings walked the rock path leading to their mother's house, past manicured blue plumbago bushes lined with fragrant white gardenias. The house was impressive, by anyone's standards. Their mother had received many requests from publications offering to do features on the house, but his mother always turned them down. Pali Maui could use the exposure, but her personal home was off-limits.

The double doors opened, and Christel stepped out onto the wrap-around. "What took you so long?" She waved them inside.

Katie tossed her purse on the entry table. "It's not like we had a lot of notice."

"I had to get someone to cover my shift," Aiden complained. "It's not easy to drop everything when summoned by Queen Christel."

Their older sister gave an exaggerated roll of her eyes. "Claims the Drama King of the family."

Shane lifted two open palms. "You all consider me a bum with no schedule. So, no problem here."

Christel drilled him with a look. "Yeah, about that." She gave his arm a playful punch as he moved inside.

"Seriously," Shane said. "What's up? Where's Mom?"

"I'm right here," Ava said, entering the room. She had a large pile of folded clothes in her arm—their dad's jeans and jackets, his button-down shirts. She'd gathered his swim trunks, his board shorts, and rash guard shirts. Christel quickly moved to relieve her of them and set the pile on the end of the crème-colored wrap-around sofa.

"I asked Christel to summon you. I'm packing your father's

things. They will all be out of here by tonight. Before the moving trucks arrive, I wanted to give you all a chance to retrieve anything you wish to keep. Mementos, things that might mean something to you."

"Moving trucks?" Katie said, surprised. "You're getting rid of Dad's things? Like, everything? So...so soon?"

Ava straightened her spine and gave a firm nod. "Yes."

"It's not so soon, really," Christel said, coming to her mother's rescue. "All the grief books say people need to move at their own pace. What is right for one might not be the ticket for another."

Katie heaved a big sigh. "Queen Christel now thinks she's Dr. Phil."

Aiden lifted a shirt off the top of the pile, stared at it.

"Do you want that, son?" Ava asked.

"No, I—" Aiden quickly re-folded it and put the shirt back. "I was just looking." He and Shane exchanged glances.

"Why now, Mom?" Shane asked. "I mean, it's a big job and all. Are you sure you're up for this? It's only been a couple of months after..." He let his words drift, unable to finish.

Again, Ava firmly nodded. "I don't expect you kids to fully understand, but it's time for me to move on."

Christel ran her hand through the side of her short bob. "That's a good sign, Mom."

Katie turned to her sister and huffed. "Would you give it a rest?"

"Girls," Ava admonished them with a look not so unlike the ones she'd given them over the years when they'd argued over bathroom usage and who got to borrow the car and whose turn it was to do the dishes after dinner. "My mind is made up. Now, all I need for you children to do is pull the items you want before it all goes."

She beckoned them to follow her into her bedroom, which was stacked with more clothes. Their dad's shoes and toiletries were lined up against the wall. His books were stacked next to the bed. Even his reading glasses were ready to be taken away.

The sight seemed to rattle Aiden. His face turned mottled and pale. "Wow. This makes everything so...final."

Four siblings stood silent for several long moments. Even Christel—who'd been their mother's advocate, swallowed hard as the memories of their childhood—their very lives—hung heavily in the room that still smelled like their father.

Shane swallowed the lump in his throat. "Well, if this has to be done now, then let's get to it."

The task was a massive one and took many hours. Each of them selected a few items that they wanted as keepsakes. The rest was left for the men who would be showing up to pack and cart the remaining possessions away. Alani's son, Ori, ran *Ka Hale a Ke Ola* Resource Center. He'd make sure the items went to people who needed them.

Christel chose some of her father's leather-bound business books. Much of the content was now antiquated, given they were published well before the digital age, but she had fond memories of her father holding the books in his hand and poring over the pages with a glass of bourbon on the table beside him.

Katie picked out a pair of cufflinks he often wore and a half-empty bottle of his favorite cologne. She removed the cap and sniffed. Tears immediately formed as her father's signature scent hit her nostrils.

Aiden wanted his surfboard and his sunglasses. Shane chose his custom-painted motorcycle helmet.

"What all are you keeping, Mom?" Katie asked.

They all turned their eyes on their mother, waiting.

Ava took a deep breath. "I—I'm keeping my good memories," she told them, her voice cracking on the last word. "Everything else, I'm letting go."

19

Ori banged on his sister's front door. No answer. He pounded again and poked the doorbell repeatedly. Finally, a muffled sound came from the other side, and the door slowly opened. He pushed through, nearly knocking his sister over.

"Hey, come on in," Mia said sarcastically.

"Cut the crap," he barked. "What's going on with you? Mom filled me in. What the—"

She held up open palms as if to deflect the onslaught of his questions. "I don't need more judgment." Tears filled her eyes.

"More judgment? You were having an affair with a married man. Not just any married man. With Lincoln Briscoe." He shook his head in disbelief. "How in the world did you think this would end, Mia? How could you be so stupid? Did you believe you could do such a thing and it would never be found out?"

Mia buried her head in her hands. "It doesn't matter now. He's dead." She looked up, crushed. "And I loved him."

Lincoln's dead, in part, because of you. Ori bit down on the words that he'd promised not to speak. But the fact remained, had Lincoln not been driving home from Hana on that rainy night, he might not have had the fatal accident. He would still be alive. In light of all that, he said nothing. He simply moved to her sofa and sunk into the cushions while his teeth sunk into his tongue.

"Ori, if you came to make me feel worse—that is not possible. I couldn't be more miserable. I know what I did was wrong. I—I don't even know how we let it get that far. But we did."

Ori grabbed her hand and pulled her down beside him. "Spill. I want to know everything."

"I'm not sure—"

"Everything," he repeated. He was not cross, but he was firm. "You need to come clean, Mia. Start talking."

Her lips trembled as she pushed the first words from her mouth. "As you know, my dream was always to start my own hotel someday." She looked to the ceiling as if for strength to continue. "I suppose I got ahead of myself, but I saw online that there were opportunities for start-up capital. On a lark, I clicked and read more. The company was in Honolulu and was looking for people like me—people who had the skill set, the know-how, and the drive, but lacked finances."

Mia drew a pain-filled deep breath. "So, I reached out. One of the principles, Greer Latham, flew over and met with me. The thing took off so fast it made my head spin. He wanted proformas, revenue projections, competitive analyses, and marketing budgets. I knew almost immediately I was in over my head. The only thing I could think to do was to call Lincoln."

"Why Lincoln? Why not Dad?" Ori asked.

"Our father is many things. But a businessman is not one of them. He barely knows how to tweet and has no idea what

LinkedIn even is. Besides, I was wary of letting anyone know that I was even pursuing such a lofty thing. What if I failed?"

"So, Lincoln came to your aid?"

"Yes. He agreed to keep this between us. We met several nights, and he was such a help. He showed me what I needed to focus on, helped me prepare the necessary documents, and helped me practice my big pitch. I was a nervous wreck, but with his encouragement, I determined I would at least give it my best shot." She looked at her brother, her face filled with emotion. "I wanted this so badly."

"And, then?"

"Then came the in-person meeting. Like I said, Greer Latham flew in from Honolulu, and we met in the bar in the lobby of the Hyatt where I work. We shared a couple of cocktails while I described my proposal. He was so attentive and curious, asked all the right questions. After a couple of hours, he gave a clear indication that he was interested in moving forward to the next level." She paused. "That's when the trouble began."

"Trouble?"

"Yes. That is when that jerk made his move. He placed his hand on my leg. When I cautiously pulled away, he didn't take the hint. He got a little more aggressive and laid his room key on the bar, making his intentions clear."

Mia stood up, began pacing. "I told him in no uncertain terms that I was not agreeable, even when he dangled that my lack of cooperation would jeopardize the deal." She stopped and turned her full attention on Ori. "What he didn't know is that Lincoln was sitting at the end of the bar. He was there to give me moral support...anonymously."

"What happened then?"

"Lincoln jumped up and came to my rescue. I won't tell you what he said, but his message was clear. The entire deal folded, of course. I was crushed when I realized I'd been played. There was likely no intention to ever grant me a business partnership. At least not one with no strings attached."

Through the window, they watched the palm fronds swaying in the breeze.

Mia sighed. "I'm embarrassed to admit my reaction. I was crushed and sobbed like a baby. Lincoln took hold of my arm and we headed upstairs to a vacant room where I could collect myself outside of the gazing eyes of hotel guests and my coworkers."

"You went to a hotel room with Lincoln? Alone? Oh, Mia."

Tears streamed down Mia's face. She shrugged and looked away, no longer able to meet his scrutiny. "He held me as I fell apart...one thing led to another. The details don't really matter except that we'd spent so much time together that somewhere along the way he'd quit being our friends' dad, someone I'd grown up knowing. Instead, he'd become a man who understood me, who admired my abilities and was in my corner. He was charming, smart and nothing like the guys my own age. He wasn't the man I'd grown up knowing...he was this new Lincoln. He was holding me, and I wanted him. I did," she admitted, swiping at her face with the back of her arm. "I wanted him."

Her face crumpled as she turned back. "Mom is right. What looked so good turned out to be the end of me."

Ori leapt from the sofa, enfolded his sister in his arms. "It's not the end, Mia. Far from it. What you did was wrong. You hurt a lot of people, including yourself. But you can rise from this. Start over. Make things right again."

That's when he saw the suitcases. "You're packed. Are you going somewhere?"

She pulled from his embrace. "The best thing I can do for everyone right now is to leave. I've resigned my position here and am taking a position in San Diego. It's a stepdown in the

Hyatt organization, but that matters very little right now. I just need to go."

She was having trouble breathing. Panic had a good, strong hold on her.

He expected her to be stronger, to try harder, to believe she could turn from the wrong she'd done and be forgiven. Ori grasped his twin sister's face in his hands. "You can't run from this. You can't. You have to stay and make things right."

"Really? And how do you propose I do that, Ori? How do I undo the damage?" His sister was full-on crying now, her heart seeming to break wide open. "Should I march up to Ava's door and simply knock? Spill my guts and tell her what I did? Tell her I am responsible for Lincoln's death and the death of her marriage? Do you think that will make everything better for her?" She pulled back with disgust. "And what about Christel? My best friend growing up. Do you think she'll ever forgive me for sleeping with her father? For what I did to her mother and family? Not to mention our own parents. They are deeply ashamed. Mom will never get over what I've done." She shook her head angrily. "Don't be foolish. You know I'm right. I just need to go."

Ori realized there was no changing her mind. She'd left her job and her mind was made up. His sister was moving to San Diego, at least for now. "Please, just assure me you'll go and talk with Mom and Dad before you leave. Promise me, Mia. It will crush them even worse if you just leave without a word." He looked at her with pleading eyes. "Do it for me?"

Mia drew a deep breath and slowly nodded in defeat. "For you."

20

"Is she still asleep?" Katie asked as she shut the front door and walked into her living room.

Jon looked up from the laptop perched on his lap. "Yeah. I was sweating it, wondering if you'd get back before Willa came down."

Katie checked her watch. It was nearly eleven in the morning. She didn't like Jon allowing their daughter to sleep in that late. This morning that had worked in her favor. "Where's Noelle?"

Jon shut his laptop and slid it to the sofa beside him. "I gave her a bath, and she ate some banana bread for breakfast. She's in the bedroom playing with that doll that wets all over."

He'd been very vocal about how he disliked that doll, but Katie thought the way their tiny daughter worked so hard to diaper her pretend baby was adorable. The fact their older daughter might be doing that task for real in a few months nearly choked her.

Jon rubbed at the back of his neck. "So, I'm going to have to get over to the restaurant soon. Should we wake her?"

Katie nodded. "I'll do it."

She headed down the hall. It had been a wretched morning already and was about to worsen. She rapped on her daughter's bedroom door then eased it open.

Willa was already awake, sitting on the edge of her bed. Her daughter looked so young, so vulnerable. It was all Katie could do to keep from tearing up. She was both compassionate and really, *really* angry.

Katie was a good mother. She'd had the talk with her daughter very early. Pressed Willa to come to her before she took any kind of step in that direction. Yes, she'd pushed the notion of abstinence and all the reasons why sex outside marriage was not best—religious implications included. Still, she knew teens often did not follow their parents' advice, especially when it came to such matters.

"I need you to get dressed and come downstairs. Your father and I need to talk with you." Katie watched for a reaction, some signal that her daughter might clue in to her parents' discovery. Willa simply pulled her hair back and knotted it at the base of her neck. "Why? What's up?"

"Just come down. Quickly," she added.

Downstairs, Jon was pacing. Katie gave him a stern look. "Get it together. We have to have a united front here."

Her husband rubbed the back of his neck again. "I'll follow your lead."

Of course, he would. That was Jon's way. An annoying characteristic that often worked in her favor.

Willa made her way down the stairs, dressed but without shoes. "I'm starving."

Jon parked his hands on his hips. "You'll get fed after we talk."

Katie threw him a warning look. This discussion could not come across as a confrontation, despite the fact it was just that. She wished Willa had come to her before taking such a step, but certainly, this entire situation raised an important set of questions. Why hadn't her daughter come to her upon learning she might be pregnant? Why had she taken that test without confiding in her, without allowing her mother to come alongside and support her?

"Sit down, honey." Katie motioned to a spot at the table. She nodded for Jon to sit as well. "You know, don't you, that you can come to us with anything? I mean, anything."

Willa looked confused. "Yeah, I know."

"And your mother and I are always here to support you," Jon added.

"Something is obviously on your mind. Just spill," Willa told them, now clearly exasperated. "What did I do?"

"Oh, honey. You didn't do anything. I mean..." She looked to Jon for support. He bobbed his head up and down. "I'm just a little confused as to why..."

"We know you're pregnant," Jon blurted. He ran a hand through the top of his hair.

Katie turned on him, gave him a look that said she'd deal with him later. She opened her mouth to speak, but Willa immediately cut her off.

"Pregnant? I'm not pregnant!" Willa shoved her chair back, stood. "You thought I was pregnant?"

Jon's face turned sheepish. "I found the positive test. In the guest bathroom."

Willa's face paled. "It's—that test, well...it isn't mine."

Katie's breath caught. Relieved, she stood as well. "Willa, it wasn't yours?" She'd heard her daughter, but her mind was spinning. She'd spent countless hours figuring out how their family would navigate this...*situation*...and now, now she was being told it didn't exist.

"No! Geez! What do you guys think of me?"

Was Willa lying now? Her anger seemed disproportionate to the accusation, considering *someone* left a positive pregnancy test in their bathroom trash. Katie gritted her teeth. "Well then, who took that test? Someone is pregnant. If not you, then who is?"

"It was positive?" Willa's gaze rushed back and forth as if putting together the disjointed pieces of a puzzle. She hesitated briefly, then folded her arms across her chest. "I'm not telling you."

Katie's emotions boiled over. She jabbed her finger at her daughter. "Oh, yes, you are indeed going to tell me who took a pregnancy test in *our* bathroom. And you will supply the information unless you don't want to leave this house except for school for the next six months." She felt her husband's hand at her back, a signal to calm down. Funny how he'd been the one nearing explosion only moments ago and how he'd slid right into the "voice of reason" role once they knew their daughter wasn't pregnant.

Willa looked to Jon, who often came to her rescue. "What your mother said. We have to know, honey. And if that means calling your friends' parents..."

Willa sucked a breath. "You wouldn't dare."

"Oh, yes, we would," Katie assured her daughter. "If we're going to come to a battle of wills, you better be fully armed." Moments ticked past.

Katie suddenly remembered coming home and finding that new girl at the house. Amanda? Yes, that was her name. Willa had gone on and on about how much she liked the girl, how she wasn't like her other friends. The new girl was really *dope*... which she understood meant impressive.

Katie understood far more than that. She'd had a friend just like Amanda back when she was in school...a girl who moved to the island and who seemed so much older. She wore the kind of clothes you'd see in a magazine, carried expensive bags, and drove a really nice car. It hadn't taken long for Katie to understand the girl's parents were rich and threw money at their daughter to assuage their guilt at not being there. Their time was occupied in business endeavors and the poor girl was pretty much left on her own.

Honestly, she felt sorry for her daughter's friend, but no way was she going to allow any bad influences in Willa's life. She was not so naïve as to believe she could bubble wrap her daughter and protect her from all the bad things that would likely come her way. Still, she didn't need her impressionable young daughter thinking dating and having sex was glamorous.

"I'll need Amanda's parents' names," she told Willa. "Unless there is someone else who was recently in our home and the test belongs to them." Katie stood determined, locked eye-to-eye with Willa.

Her daughter melted into resignation. "Fine! Have it your way. You'll only be costing me a friend...and my reputation at school. You're turning me into a snitch."

Willa recited their names and Katie made note of them on a piece of paper. She'd call and make arrangements to meet with Amanda's parents soon and make sure they were aware of their daughter's situation. She hated to admit it, but every cell in her body was relieved to pass that heavy baton onto someone else.

Willa was not pregnant.

Finally, something positive had happened this week.

21

Christel finished reviewing the month-end financials—the cash flow statement, the balance sheet, and the important profit and loss figures. She prided herself on how she was both able to delegate tasks to their small staff and maintain responsibility over every aspect of the accounting functions. Businesses often suffered when the person in charge abdicated close supervision.

With the deal with Latham now behind them, a new partner would have to be scouted. New marketing materials produced. This time she'd stay involved. She'd made a mistake thinking Katie could handle something like that without her.

Christel closed her laptop, and grabbed her now tepid coffee, and moved for the kitchenette. She dumped the cold brown liquid down the sink and rinsed out her mug. Had she even eaten today?

The only thing in the cupboard was an open carton of stale Fig Newtons. Even the edges were crusty. She shrugged and ate one anyway.

With all the added projects on her plate, her work hours extended far past normal. As a result, her social life had suffered, as had her ability to sleep soundly. Her father's passing had forced so many changes. New banking documents, revised corporate and loan structures, and a redistribution of projected earnings—all took careful managing to reduce tax obligations whenever possible.

Katie had accused her of neglecting time with her family—and especially their mom. That wasn't true. She was at Pali Maui every day, often having conversations with her mother about a multitude of business matters. And hadn't they all just had a family meeting? Like her siblings, she'd dropped everything and shown up.

Yet, her mother was hurting, she could tell. As always, the woman she most admired was powering through, determined to not allow anything—not even the loss of her spouse—to hinder her ability to function at high capacity. Many said she took after her mother in that regard...a compliment she savored.

There were those who had claimed her mother was not dealing with her grief. Especially Katie and Alani. They'd said the same when Christel went through her divorce two years ago. While painful, moving on had been necessary. No one benefited from sinking too far inside their head.

Christel grabbed her phone from her desk, checked messages—answering some and ignoring others. She pushed the phone deep inside her pants pocket and headed out. Minutes later, she was on her mom's doorstep.

She knocked lightly before pushing the door open. "Mom?" she called out. "It's Christel."

"Hi, honey. I'm in here," her mother called back from the kitchen, where she was pouring granola into a bowl. She waved Christel in as she grabbed a pineapple and a knife. "Want some, honey?"

"Sure," Christel told her. She'd prefer bacon, eggs, and a stack of pancakes, but beggars couldn't be choosers.

Her mom moved for the refrigerator. "You get all the month-end done?" She pulled a container of milk and brought it over to the kitchen island.

Christel turned from her and retrieved two spoons from a drawer, but not before noticing the dark circles under her mother's eyes. Christel swallowed hard and found her way to a barstool. "Yup. All done. We're in great shape. I think we can talk about going forward with upgrading the conveyors in the fall."

Her mom nodded. "I'm not sure I told you, but your dad had several large life insurance policies. We should make use of those funds."

Christel shook her head. "That's your money, Mom. Maybe you could actually take a vacation and go somewhere. It would do you good to get away." Even as she made the suggestion, she knew what the answer would be.

"Oh, honey. I don't have time to get away right now."

All you have now is time, Mom, she wanted to say. But Christel settled for, "So, Mom. I've been working night and day this past week. I think it'd do us both good to take a break today. Maybe go hiking? Or, we could take the kayaks out to Maluaka Beach and make a run at Turtle Town and check out the *ke ola moana*. I heard that in addition to the sea turtles, schools of angelfish and butterflyfish are especially active right now. What do you say, Mom?"

"Ah, honey. I'd love to. Raincheck?" Her mother poured milk over the two bowls of granola and shoved one in front of Christel before plunging her spoon into her own. "Tell you what. Let's walk the fields. Miguel and the field hands got two truckloads of pineapple tops yesterday, and they planted them this morning. I know it's not necessary, but I'd like to check it out."

Pali Maui collected scrap pineapple tops from all the major

resorts on Maui and used those to replant the pineapple fields. The early hours after planting were critical.

"Sure, Mom. At least it'll get us out in the fresh air." Christel would have much preferred getting her mom away from Pali Maui, but her mother had always had precision focus. Again, a character trait she, too, had been accused of having.

There was a time she'd have given anything to be wife and mother, but that hadn't panned out. After the divorce, she sank deeply into her work—lucky to have it. It was her saving grace.

When they'd finished eating, they grabbed their sunglasses and headed out to the fields. Earlier burns had made the soil soft and rich and ready for planting. Tiny pineapple crowns sprouted up from neatly spaced rows for as far as they could see. Many months from now, the fruit would be harvested, processed, and shipped.

"Did I tell you Mig was able to find the additional workers we needed?" her mother asked as they skirted the edge of the fields. In the distance, a boom harvester slowly made its way through a field ready for harvest.

Christel took in the sweet aroma in the air, the way the ripened fruit emitted its signature fragrance. "No. That's good news." Lack of dedicated workers was a frequent issue they faced.

"And it looks like we are going to be invited to bid the DeBoer contract."

"Oh, Mom. That's wonderful! Things are really starting to fall together."

Many of their competitors had moved their fruit operations to Costa Rica to avoid taxes and costs associated with doing business in the United States. Because their costs were lower, they could cut prices to gain market share. Pali Maui had diversified but struggled nonetheless to counter these measures.

Her mom's face grew pensive as she stopped near the center of the field where short, spiky, green plants and rich dark earth surrounded them. "Honey, I don't tell you enough, but I am so glad to have you here at Pali Maui. Especially now."

"Mom, how are you? Really?"

"I'm okay," she said quietly.

Christel didn't believe her, especially given the look of exhaustion that played across her face and the deep purplish half-moons beneath her mother's beautiful hazel eyes. "Are you sleeping?"

"Sometimes," her mother admitted with a one-shouldered shrug. "But then, I've always had trouble with that. One of the things that comes with getting older." She winked, bravely trying to put on a happy face.

Christel placed her arms around her mom's shoulders and gave her a tight squeeze. "It'll get better, I promise."

Back at the house, Christel offered to prepare lunch. "I can make a Cobb salad," she said, rummaging through the fridge.

Her mom tossed her jacket on the back of the sofa. "We just ate."

"That was several hours ago," Christel told her. "Besides, it looks like you're losing weight. It won't hurt you to consume a few more calories." When Jay left her and moved back to Alaska, she had no appetite whatsoever. When your spirit was broken, it seemed your body shut down and reserved all pleasure, physical and otherwise, for another time—a point down the road when your senses woke back up after crawling in bed and pulling the covers over your emotions. A warm bath, a good meal...nothing mattered. Her mother, while strong, was likely in a similar state. "Better yet, Mom, let's wander over to *No Ke 'Oi* and see what Jon has on special."

She reluctantly agreed, and they walked the short distance to the restaurant. The maître d seated them at an open-air table overlooking the golf course. "I'll be right back," Christel told her mom, leaving her to enjoy the view.

"Hey, Jon!" Christel peeked her head inside the kitchen and waved at her brother-in-law. "Anything good today?"

He grinned and wiped his hands on a towel tucked into his apron belt. "Anything good? That's like asking if the Mona Lisa is a great painting. Of course, I have something good." He pushed her out of his kitchen. "You go back and sit, and I'll surprise you."

True to his word, Jon showed up at the table minutes later with two platters of shrimp won tons with macadamia nut sauce and side salads. He also had Hookipa Sunset cocktails delivered to the table.

Ava held up her hand. "Stop. We both have to go back to work."

"C'mon, Mom," Christel urged. "Let's live a little."

Jon grinned at them. "And when that's done, I have a piece of coconut chiffon cake waiting."

Over the course of the next hour, the two of them indulged. They even ordered a second cocktail. "I suppose there's nothing so terribly pressing that we have to get right back," her mom admitted.

It was so nice to see her mother smile. It made Christel feel good inside, knowing that her mom's spirits were lifted a bit, even if only for a while. Frankly, the downtime was not hurting her, either.

When Jon came to check on them, Christel noted she hadn't seen Katie's car.

Jon nodded. "Yeah, we had a slight family issue. She went to talk to Willa's friend's mother." Before he could tell them more, Katie's car came into sight. "There she is now. I'll let her fill you in."

Katie swept in, looking flushed. "Oh, I am so glad to see you both." She turned to her husband. "I'll have what they are having. Hold the food."

He grinned and leaned to kiss her cheek. "How'd it go?"

"Not well," she told him. She slid into a chair at the table. "I swear, that daughter of mine is killing me about three times a day." She motioned for Jon to sit, and she filled her mom and sister in. "You can only imagine how Jon and I felt, thinking Willa was pregnant."

Jon nodded. "I grew a bunch of gray hair in a matter of a few hours."

The waiter arrived at the table with Katie's cocktail. She thanked him and took a quick sip before continuing. "Well, I went to talk to Amanda's mother. That was a big mistake."

"What do you mean?" Ava asked.

"Well, for one thing, she's mean as spit. Seems her little darling denied everything. Told her mother our Willa was lying and that the test was hers." She took another generous sip of her cocktail. "Well, I know who I saw coming out of the bathroom that day. Besides that, Willa has been a handful lately, but she's not a liar. In fact, I mistook her embarrassment as guilt."

"Embarrassment?" Christel asked.

"Yeah," Katie said, swiping the moisture from the side of her glass. "I realized later that she was embarrassed we thought she was sexually active."

Jon agreed. "She knows better. And she's not one to lie. Especially about something like this."

"Well, when I pushed about what we'd learned, Amanda's mother told me to mind my own business!" Katie huffed. "Like I was trying to pry. I was simply doing what any responsible mother and adult would do. I wanted to make sure she knew her daughter might need her help." She shook her head in disgust. "That's why we have the issues we have today. Parents don't do their jobs. I mean, life can dish some pretty hard stuff. Hiding from the truth is never the answer."

Ava fingered her empty martini glass. "Oh, I don't know..."

They all turned to her.

"What?" Christel asked, puzzled.

Her mother seemed to realize what she'd said and quickly retracted her statement. "What I meant is, sometimes the only way to make it through is to sweep today's hurts under tomorrow's rug." Her face broke into a weak smile. "The poor woman may need to get her feet underneath her before she can fully admit the truth...even to herself."

22

"All finished, Mrs. Kané." A big black man with gray dreadlocks wearing a blue jumpsuit wiped his oily fingers off on a rag.

"Thanks, Cliff." Alani quickly finished counting the new shipment of glassware and noted the inventory on her clipboard before moving in his direction. "So, it was the compressor, like you thought?" The man standing before her was the best in the business. Everyone on the island knew he could fix anything. And in record time.

Cliff nodded. "Yeah, mon. But, you're good to go now," he told her in a thick Jamaican accent. Grateful, she signed off on the repair manifest, then instructed her employees to restock the cooler with the food items currently iced down in large containers in the back room. Cliff and his maintenance crew had been there all morning after their main refrigerator unit went on the blink and needed repair. The unexpected event had left her behind. Tonight's luau was sold out, and she still had so much to do.

Hours before, a whole pig had been wrapped in banana

leaves and burlap and nested on a rack over a pit filled with hot cinders. The pit had been covered with a sheet of tin with a thick layer of dirt over the top. Just before the food would be placed on the guest tables, the meat would be dug up and served along with all the other menu items—lomi salmon, pineapple rice, chicken katsu, and baked mahi-mahi. And that was only the entrees. There would also be an open bar and a dessert table, compliments of the corporate sponsor, a travel agency that catered to high-end travelers who expected only the best.

When the kitchen duties were under control, Alani turned her attention to the preparations for the stage show. The performers would be arriving soon, and they'd need to do a soundcheck. There would be costume adjustments and unexpected changes to the program to accommodate employees who failed to show for one reason or another. She couldn't count on both hands the numbers of times one of their firedancers called in with an excuse at the last minute.

The fact Alani had pulled off more authentic Hawaiian luaus than anyone on the island didn't mean she escaped the building nerves that showed up before start time. A million parts and pieces needed to come together, and the pressure on her chest often felt like a heart attack.

Tonight was no different...and in some ways, her emotions grew more intense.

Alani couldn't get Mia off her mind. She'd wept off and on ever since their confrontation, replaying the conversation in her mind and rehearsing all the things she could've said or should've said. She'd had no practice at such a thing and worried she'd done it all wrong. Despite planning her words carefully, Alani had lost her temper. She'd been anything but gracious. She was stinking mad at her daughter, and it had shown.

Even so, Alani had so hoped Mia would...what? Say she was

sorry? Claim it was all a horrible misunderstanding, that she really hadn't had an affair with Lincoln after all?

Had she been too tough on her daughter? Or not enough?

Tears suddenly formed. Emotions had run high, and anger poured. Righteous anger, but still. She'd wanted to say all the right things. She wanted things to be different.

Alani felt that little shadow behind her eyes and knew she could *want* all she wanted...sometimes, words simply fail.

She wiped her cheek and headed for the dressing room. Minutes later, she reappeared wearing her *muumuu*. A line was already forming at check-in and she moved to greet the crowd.

It was then that she saw her...Mia.

Her daughter stood in the distance, leaning against the trunk of a palm tree. The dark green fronds swung in the breeze like they hadn't a care in the world. The same could not be said for the look on her daughter's face.

Alani quickly glanced around before walking in that direction. "Mia?" she uttered as she neared.

Her daughter was crying. She looked a wreck, and her clothes hung off her lithe body. Alarm snaked through Alani's system. Her daughter looked like she hadn't slept in days.

"Mia! What is it?" Alani stopped herself from rushing forward. "Are you okay?"

"Am I okay?" her daughter repeated, her voice choked with emotion. "No. I'm not okay."

Alani placed a hand over her chest, feeling the erratic beating of her own heart.

"Momma, I am—" Mia's words faltered. Several long seconds passed before she seemed able to breathe. She made her voice as strong as she could make it. "I am leaving."

"Leaving?" Alani's heart now crept up in her throat, choking off her air. "Where are you going?" Out of instinct, she reached and touched her daughter's arm.

Mia flinched. "It is best." She told her of her plans to move off-island and to San Diego. Ori would drive her to the airport in the morning. "I took a transfer."

"Oh, Mia." Alani looked over at her daughter, her gaze sharp and assessing. "Mia, you have to make this right. You can't just run. You cannot escape what you've done by simply changing addresses."

"We both know there is nothing I can do to alter any of this. I can never make what happened better. Beyond the affair, Lincoln is dead. I am responsible for all of it." Mia's lips trembled. "I am ashamed that I hurt you—and Dad," she mumbled. "Make things right?" She shook her head violently. "Some things can never be made right."

Alani realized her daughter was having trouble breathing. Panic had a good, strong hold on her. "I was in love with him," she confessed. "Yet, somewhere along the way, I'd forgotten that some kinds of love have a dark underside." Her body shook, now racked with sobs. "Love blinded me, Momma. I became reckless and selfish. I wounded our friends and brought *hilahila* upon our family."

Alani took hold of Mia by the shoulders, relieved to finally hear her daughter's confession of guilt. "You listen to me, my precious one. You did a terrible thing. But you are not a terrible person." Her daughter had just handed Alani her wounded heart, wrapped it up, and placed it in her hands, bleeding. She knew she must not be careless with it.

She lifted Mia's chin with her ample fingers. "Darling, girl. From the moment the good Lord formed you in the deepest measure of my womb, you were a part of me. There is simply nothing you could ever do to make me love you more than I always have—and nothing you could do to make me love you less." Alani drew a deep, quivering breath. "You are going to have to trust my heart on this. Your father and I both adore you, Mia. That never changes. No matter what you have done."

The ground appeared to dissolve beneath her daughter's

feet. Alani's unwavering love and support was a tidal wave, whooshing without warning. Mia folded onto the grass, overcome with emotion.

Alani crumbled next to her and held her, rocking her precious daughter as her shame poured out. "You are loved, Mia. Nothing changes that," she repeated.

One thing, she saw clearly. Her daughter had much healing to do. Mia would have to find a way to reconcile her ability to fall from high places into the pit from hell. She would have to find a way to forgive herself, pick up the splintered pieces of her life, and become whole again.

When the tears were exhausted, Mia pulled out of her mother's embrace and lifted. She dug in her purse and retrieved a sealed envelope. "Will you give this to Ava? When it's time?"

"Yes, Mia. I will do that." Alani said quietly, wishing she didn't feel compelled to make that promise. She brushed Mia's long dark hair from her shoulders.

She, too, wanted to cry, was desperate for a way to release her own pain, but no tears came. Only the solace that her shattered daughter was sorry for what she'd done kept Alani steady on the shifting sand. It would have to be enough.

In the end, Mia would leave the island. Her mother's heart told her she had to let her girl go, hoping that, someday, her precious daughter would return.

23

Aiden stood in front of his locker at the MEMA and placed his official jacket on the hook inside. It had been a long day. As the official liaison between Maui Emergency Management Administration and the volunteer Search and Rescue unit, his days often started well before dawn and ended hours after the sun went down. Today had been one of those days.

An incident at Honolua Bay had prompted several calls into the station reporting a group of teens had ignored the signs and were in the water near where there'd been a shark sighting. A day earlier, a young girl took a hit to the leg by an apparent tiger shark, causing lacerations to her calf. A riptide near Kauai swept a seven-year-old several yards away from his parents, who could not reach him. Thankfully, he wore a life jacket and was rescued. Two hikers got lost on Waikamoi Trail and were found, thanks to the SAR team. All of that had taken place before noon.

His phone buzzed. He lifted it to find a text from Katie, reminding him it was family game night. He groaned. Shaking his tired head, he quickly texted back that he'd forgotten and was going to have to pass. That prompted an immediate phone call.

"What do you mean you have to pass?" Katie demanded as soon as he answered. "We all agreed we needed to support Mom through these next weeks and months. She shouldn't spend night after night alone."

"Katie, I'm dead on my feet," he argued.

"We all have stuff, Aiden. But it's game night. We all agreed that we would make the effort. Mom needs us. We can't bail on her. Especially right now."

"C'mon, you can turn off the firehose of guilt. I know Mom needs us. I only wish it wasn't tonight." He shut his locker door. "Can't we reschedule?"

Several seconds passed. He stared at his phone. Nothing.

"Wait, I have another call," Katie finally answered. "Let me call you right back." His sister hung up without waiting for his response.

Almost immediately, his phone buzzed. Another text. This time from Christel. *"C'mon. If I have to go, you do, too."*

Aiden rolled his eyes. He couldn't fight both of them. *"Fine. I'll be there. But keep the evening short. We're not choosing Monopoly."*

Monopoly was his sisters' favorite board game. Despite their sweet looks, the two could be ruthless when it came to vying for Boardwalk and Park Place. He and Shane never won when pitted against the two of them—not when they were relegated to the railroads and properties like Baltic Avenue.

A shrill whistle came from the front. Aiden pocketed his phone and headed in that direction to find a woman standing in the reception area with her finger and thumb tucked in her lips, ready to let another blast.

"Can I help you?" Aiden glanced around the empty reception area. "Sorry, Hazel must've stepped away." He turned back to the girl. She had long black hair that hung well below her shoulders and wore a baseball cap backward. Her arms were heavily tattooed. Were those...*tigers*?

"What can I do for you?" he repeated. She was stunning, in a dangerous way. A tough chick with a figure that could crumble the rock formations at Nakalele. Seriously.

"Yeah, I'm here for the job," she told him.

Aiden frowned. "Job?"

She reached in her back pocket and pulled out a folded paper, opened it. "Yeah, the assistant to the liaison something." She shrugged and handed the paper to him. "I'm not really into labels, but I talked to the director last week, and he hired me."

Aiden's eyebrows shot up. "You talked to Mike?"

She nodded. "Yup. Mike Purdue. He told me to come on in. I had the job."

Aiden rubbed the back of his neck. "I—I'm a bit surprised. I mean, I'm the liaison. I'm sure Mike would have discussed all this with me before hiring—"

"Look, call him if you like. But he did hire me. I just need someone to show me around."

Jud Fogleman entered the room. He popped the top on his can of soda. "I'll do it. I just clocked off, but I don't have any plans or anything." There was no mistaking the eager expression on his coworker's face.

Aiden glanced between the two of them. "Look, hold on just a second. I'll be right back." He hurried back to his locker while scrolling his phone for Mike's number. His boss picked up on the first ring. "Mike, we need to talk."

"So, you met her?"

"Met her? She's in the front office, and I didn't even know you'd hired anyone."

"Yeah, about that...well, we both know the hours you've been putting in. And the stress you've been under ever since your dad's accident."

"My dad's accident has nothing to do with anything," Aiden

barked. He took a deep breath, toned down his approach. "Look, I wish you would have discussed this with me before jumping forward. I should have had the opportunity to weigh in on the new hire, if that was on the horizon. I don't even know this girl."

"She's well qualified," Mike explained. "Her name is Megan McCord. She's an Army brat, has lived all over. Most recently, she spent a year in Pacific Bay, a little town in Oregon. She worked for a friend of mine named Cameron Davis. He highly recommended her."

Aiden shook his head. It was a done deal. "Fine. I'll do what I can to support her orientation."

"Thanks, Aiden. I knew the transition might be difficult for you, given all the stress you've been under. And, yes, I should have talked with you first. I knew if I didn't scoop her up, someone would. She's going to be a great asset. You'll see."

Aiden had to refrain from arguing. He was not under stress. Sure, a death in the family took a toll, especially when you were on the rescue team. Clear rules were in place against anyone responding to an incident involving a family member, but no one knew that was the case until it was too late. While difficult, he'd dealt with the situation just fine.

"Okay, sure." He told Mike goodbye and hung up, then returned to the front office.

The new girl and Jud were laughing. Aiden cleared his throat, interrupting their exchange. "Yeah, so...just talked with Mike. Looks like we're good to go."

The new hire smiled back at him like she never doubted for a minute how the deal would go down. Aiden couldn't bring himself to smile back. He didn't really care for people who were smug, even if they looked like her. "So, let's give you the tour."

24

"You're late," Katie announced as Aiden entered the kitchen.

Aiden nodded. "Yeah, work issues."

Ava moved to join her son and pulled him into a tight embrace. "Hey, honey. Have you eaten?" Without waiting for a reply, she pushed a plate into his hands, then moved for the oven, donned some mitts, and pulled a pan of steaming-hot lasagna from the rack. She placed it on the counter. "C'mon, everyone. Dinner's ready."

The entire family said she made the best lasagna, a point she couldn't argue. The recipe came from her father, who claimed it came from his grandmother. Homemade sheets of pasta layered with sauce from fresh tomatoes and basil simmered on the stove for hours. Grated cheese in heaping amounts and a secret ingredient—a sprinkle of sugar between each layer.

The dish was their family's go-to comfort food.

Despite the stack of plates next to her, Christel slid onto a barstool, grabbed a fork, and dug into the corner of the pan of lasagna. She lifted the bite to her mouth, nearly burning her tongue.

Katie followed suit and laid hold of her own fork, digging into the pan. Shane handed a fork to Aiden and dug smack dab into the gooey middle of the pan. Aiden liked the crispy edges. He puffed his cheeks out and tried to cool the lasagna already in his mouth.

Ava shrugged and returned the stack of plates to the cupboard.

It was moments like this that saved her—made her forget Lincoln's betrayal, even if momentary. Despite her strict vow to move on and leave the hurt behind, the volcano within her soul continued to rumble all too often. When those times came and her emotions spewed, the eruption left her feeling unstable. She had to force herself to remember what she still had—a flourishing business, friends, and a stellar reputation, and most of all—a family she adored. They adored her, too. She knew that. That was a lot. And it would be enough.

"So, Aiden. What exactly held you up tonight?" Katie asked. She leaned in to get another bite.

"Don't ask," he said as he dropped onto the barstool next to his sister. Christel and Katie's eyes bore into him with expectation. Finally, he sighed and told them all about how he was heading out from work when he was thrown a curveball. A new girl showed up claiming to be a new hire, a new hire he had known nothing about. "I immediately called Mike, and he confirmed he'd hired her."

Christel drew back, surprised. "And he didn't give you a heads-up? Wow."

Aiden wasn't ready to disclose the worries his boss had about his mental disposition. He'd taken care to hide his struggles and elude examination in that regard, especially from his family. Frankly, he didn't want any of them worrying about him. He'd survived hard things before. All he had to do was muscle through. It wasn't as if he was some marshmallow over a fire, about to melt down.

Aiden scooped another bite of lasagna onto his fork. "Her name is Megan McCord. She came here from Oregon, highly recommended." The statement sounded as flat as when he had heard it. "I mean, sounds like she's qualified. Mike said it'd take the pressure off and free me up."

Ava gave her son a sympathetic nod. "Well, you have been working a lot of hours."

Aiden laughed off the comment. "Like nobody else in this family works all the time."

They all turned their heads to Shane, who jabbed his fork deep into the pasta. He held the bite midair. "Don't look at me! Uncle Jack is a slave driver."

Aiden bumped shoulders with his younger brother. "Yeah, I see the sweat dripping off your brow now."

Christel licked the sauce from her fork and moved for the sink. She turned the faucet. "So, I thought we'd play Settlers of Catan tonight."

Shane groaned. "No, not that game. I hate those brainiac things that make you think. This is entertainment, not school." He went to the refrigerator and pulled out a beer, held it up toward his brother. "You want one?"

Katie huffed. "Yes, I'll have one," she said. "In a cold mug, please."

"I keep some in the freezer," Ava pointed out. She gathered the nearly empty pan of lasagna. "Everyone get enough?"

They all nodded.

"How about a game of poker?" Aiden suggested. "We haven't played cards forever."

They all glanced at one another, unable to argue with that. Before anyone could answer in the negative, Shane quickly moved to the kitchen junk drawer and pulled it open. "Don't you keep a deck in here?"

Ava had meant to straighten that drawer and rid it of all the broken pens, the nails, and single screws Lincoln tossed in there, but the chore always fell to the bottom of her list. "I think so."

Shane dug a pack of cards from the mess and held the deck up in victory. "Bingo!" He returned to the others. "You up for getting your pride wiped all over this table?" he asked Katie.

A tiny smile nipped at the corners of her mouth, "The better question to ask is...are you?"

"Well, I'm kick butt at poker," he quickly told his sister as they all headed for the table.

"There's usually a game going every night in the student's lounge." Above, a ceiling fan paddled lazily through the warm air.

"Which might answer for your grades," Christel noted.

"That's crap. My grades are just fine."

"Language," Ava warned while filling the sink with hot sudsy water.

"Sorry, Mom." The way he looked at her left her feeling warm inside. Even in his early twenties, he was her baby.

He joined her at the sink and leaned close, lowered his voice. "Could you spot me a few twenties? I'm a little busted right now."

Christel found her way to a spot at the table and sat. "We're playing for matchsticks, Shane."

Disappointment washed over his features. "Ah, where's the fun in that?"

Christel shuffled the cards, pushed the stack to Katie. "Cut." She glanced at her mother. "Mom, let that go for now. Come play."

"No, go ahead. I'll watch."

Katie counted out matchsticks for everyone. "So, what's the game tonight?"

"Five Card Draw—nothing wild," Christel said, dealing out the cards while everyone anted up one matchstick.

Christel finished dealing, picked up her cards. From where Ava stood, she could see her daughter's hand—three queens and two kings. Christel fought to keep her eyes from going wide.

Aiden looked at his sister with amusement, cleared his throat. "Check."

Katie followed suit. "Check."

Shane studied his cards. "Me, too."

Christel adjusted her hand, placing the cards in order. She could barely contain her smile. "Okay, it'll cost you two big diamond matchsticks."

"I'll see you." Aiden pushed out two matchsticks.

Shane did the same. "Call."

Katie leaned forward, added to the pile. "I'm in."

Christel grabbed the card deck. "Okay, Shane. How many?"

"I need a little help—three."

"Three?" She shook her head in feigned sympathy. "That's unfortunate." She gave him three cards.

Aiden's face pulled into a wide grin. "One—and look out!"

"One." Christel gave him a card.

Katie studied her hand. "I'll take four."

Christel's eyebrows lifted. "Four?"

She nodded. "Four."

Christel doled out four cards to her sister, gave her another look of pity before picking up her own cards. "Well, I guess I'll play these."

Shane and Aiden exchanged glances.

"I'll check," Aiden said.

Shane studied her. "Check."

Katie rearranged her cards. "I'll bet three."

Christel cleared her throat as a warning.

Shane gave her a look. "Hey, no cheating."

Christel shrugged off his comment, gazed down at the cards in her hand and tried to act nonchalant. "I'll bet twenty." She went for her matchstick pile.

"I believe this table has a ten-match limit," Katie reminded.

"Oh, all right. All right." She pushed ten matchsticks onto the pile in the middle of the table.

Aiden laid his hand down. "I'm looking at a lonely little pair of twos and I have a strong conviction we're all going to get clobbered," he said, looking over at his oldest sister who was already gloating.

Shane let out a heavy sigh and folded. "Well, you got rid of me."

Katie leaned back in her chair, ran her hand through her hair. "Well, I think Christel's bluffing." She threw in.

"Ha!" Christel laid down her hand. "This house is about as full as you can get. Two gents. Three ladies. Read 'em and weep."

Katie dropped her fist hard on the table causing the matchsticks to vibrate.

Christel grinned. "I just picked this hand up. I almost had a heart attack when I saw those cards." She pushed her chair back and held up her empty beer can. "Anybody want another?"

Shane flung his empty can up and waved it around. "Me! Me."

Christel gave him a playful punch in the arm and shoved her pile of matchsticks over to Katie. "Keep an eye, sis. I don't trust these two."

Shane leaned back and folded his arms behind his head. "Hey, I saw something interesting today."

Katie downed the last of her beer and got up to throw the can away. Ava reached and took it from her daughter. "Here, I'll take that, honey."

Katie thanked her, then turned her attention to Shane. "So, what did you see?"

"What?"

"What did you see? You said you saw something."

His face broke into a slow grin and his chest puffed up a little. "I saw a photograph of Christel. On an online dating site."

The color drained from Katie's face. She made a cutting motion across her throat, warning her brother to drop the subject.

He didn't.

Instead, he tugged on his earlobe and grinned even more. "Yeah, seems Christel is lonely and looking for a man."

Christel stopped dead in the kitchen, her hands full of full beer cans. "Say that again."

Shane straightened his stack of matchsticks. "Apparently, she loves any movie where they spontaneously break into song. She can only eat three slices of pizza, preferably with goat cheese and garlic, and she works too much, but loves it." He leaned over his elbows on the table. "And she's looking for someone who is down to wait in line for an amazing brunch and understands the value of walking in the rain."

Katie visibly sunk in her chair.

Christel parked herself in front of her sister and let the cans drop to the table. One tipped over.

"No one open that. It might explode," Ava warned, as she went for another can to replace it. Should she step in the middle of this and stop what she feared was coming?

There was no time. Christel jabbed her fists onto her hips and stared at Katie. "What did you do?"

Katie chewed at the corner of her lip. "I—well, I just thought maybe…"

"You opened an account on an online dating service? For me?" She shook her head, incredulous. "No. No, you didn't."

Katie's fingers went to her mouth just like when she was small. "Yeah, I kinda did," she confessed.

Ava's hand went to her chest. "Oh, Katie." She then threw her youngest son a look. Some things never changed. He still enjoyed getting his sisters riled.

"Wow." Aiden reached for a can and popped the top. "Yikes."

"Why would you do something like that?" Christel demanded.

Katie shrugged. "You never date. Not since the divorce. It's time, and I thought I'd just give things a little push." She glanced between the others, looking for support. "There are some really good dating sites out there. Lots of people use them. Besides, you got nearly thirty responses in less than four hours."

Aiden rubbed the back of his neck. "Impressive."

Shane scratched at his chin. "She did use one of the better sites. I've used that one myself." He, too, shrugged. "Just saying."

"Okay, that's enough. All of you." Christel turned and jabbed her finger in Katie's direction. "You get that profile down...now!"

"Geez. All right. All right." Katie pulled her phone into her hands. Her thumbs worked across the screen furiously. She paused, waited. "There. Done."

"Thank you," Christel said. She moved back into her chair at the table. "You are a handful, you know that?"

Katie dared to smile back at her. "Maybe."

Ava wiped her hands on the kitchen towel and listened as her grown children continued their poker game and chattered on about their lives. Shane was seeing a new girl. Katie and Willa were still working out some issues related to the friend who had taken the pregnancy test. According to Katie, Jon was little help when it came to setting stricter boundaries for their young teen daughter. He disliked being a disciplinarian.

Christel and Aiden were both less forthcoming. They seemed to be okay and dealing with their father's death, but she worried. They both seemed to have become loners and buried themselves in their work. Of course, she was one to talk on that issue.

Ava folded the kitchen towel and looked around the familiar setting. This house had been Lincoln's idea. She would've been content remaining in the original residence, the house now occupied by Mig, their farm manager.

Lincoln had big dreams. This house, one of them. He'd hired a team of architects and landscapers and designers. The house was massive, by most anyone's standards—as was the budget. Back then, she'd argued their children were nearly grown. What would the two of them do with a house with eight bedrooms, two swimming pools, three separate lanai areas? While the views were stunning, this house was far too much.

They'd built more than this home together. They'd built a family. She remembered when she was pregnant with Christel, how Lincoln had placed his cheek against her swollen belly and whispered, "I'll make sure you never want for anything, sweet thing. Daddy will buy you all the dollies you can fit in your little arms." When Katie was born, he painted a bright-colored rainbow on the wall, placing a bed on either side for the girls. With emotion choking his throat, he'd told her, "Those two...they're our treasure."

She vividly recalled how excited he was when the next two babies were both boys, how he'd built a basketball hoop and court before Aiden was yet two. Lincoln had not wanted to end their family and stop at four. He would have been happy with several more, always reminding her how much he loved his own large family, where he was the youngest of six siblings. But she'd insisted their family was complete after Shane was born.

"I'm sorry," she'd told him. "I simply can't juggle everything this pineapple plantation demands and more children. It's all I can do to keep up with our family's needs now and grow this business."

Like any couple, they'd had their spats, their disagreements. Yet, they rarely out-and-out fought. She couldn't remember a time when either of them had raised their voices to the other, except only a few rare occasions.

Sure, her marriage wasn't filled with passion, at least not the kind a person read about in romance novels, but their relationship was solid, built on trust and respect. Until it wasn't. Little had she known it was all a façade...that lies and deception were the underpinning of their relationship.

Since that horrible discovery in Hana, she climbed from bed every morning, vowing to try and move on, pressing herself to leave her husband's betrayal behind and focus on what was ahead. Yet, try as she might to embrace the future, her husband's secret past kept dragging her under. The idea of him with another woman nearly choked her.

She was not an emotional woman, never had been. Lately, she often found herself staring into space, unaware of the passage of time. She didn't cry. She didn't feel...anything. She was numb.

Shane let out a yelp and placed his cards onto the table with great fanfare. "Royal flush, brothers and sisters. Royal flush!" He reached and scooped the pile of matchsticks in the center of the table into his own pile. "Consider this my shot from the bow. You're all going down."

The rest of them groaned.

Ava gazed over at her children with immense love filling her heart. She uncorked a bottle of Chenin Blanc. The bottle of French wine was from Lincoln's collection. He'd been saving it for a special occasion.

She may not have known about or even suspected her

husband's infidelity. Yet, she knew this—with everything in her, she would eventually find a way to weather this pain. More, she would not allow that pain to drift into her children's lives.

"Mom, were you expecting someone?" Christel asked as she stood and gathered the empty cans from the table. She nodded in the direction of the lane.

Ava glanced out the kitchen window to find headlights approaching. Puzzled, she crooked her head for a closer look. "It's Alani."

Her best friend's car slowly came to a stop and Alani climbed out of the passenger side. Ava drew back in surprise. "And it looks like Elta is with her."

25

Alani looked up into the dark sky pierced by thousands of tiny stars, their light a hint of hope her heart did not feel. "Elta, are you sure?"

Her husband came around the car to join her, placed his hands on both her shoulders and looked into her eyes. "We've discussed this, sweet one. Our Mia's sin is a cancer. The only way to arrest its power is to bring her actions into the light. The light always chases the darkness away."

Alani felt her eyes tear up yet again. "I'm not sure this darkness can ever be made light."

He pulled her into an embrace. She could feel his steady heart beating against her ear as he held her tightly, letting his strength become her own. "That is something that only happens by the hand of the Lord. We must trust his promises."

She so wanted to believe. Yet, if there were ever a time she wished she wasn't a pastor's wife, it might be now. Elta may be right, but what he urged came with immense risk. Ava was her best friend, her confidante, her steady female companion. The news Alani carried in her heart and the letter she held in her hand would, no doubt, wound her deeply. The thought was almost too much to bear.

"But, the children," she argued, covering her eyes with her hands. "Elta, they do not know. Ava has chosen to not disclose their father's infidelity."

Her husband drew a long breath. "As you said." He slipped his hand around her own and gently led her from the car and up the pathway leading to the Briscoes' entrance. "The light," he reminded her. Elta gave her hand a final squeeze, then rang the doorbell.

The door immediately swung open, and Ava appeared. She was dressed in white pants and a pink sleeveless top. No shoes. She held a glass of white wine in her hand. "Alani? Elta? What are you doing here?" Then, quickly added, "Come in." She punctuated her statement with a wide sweep of her hand, bidding them inside.

Alani looked to her husband for reassurance. He took her hand, and she followed him into the wide foyer and on into the main living area. She knew the room well, had spent many hours there socializing with their friends. They'd even spent a few holidays at that table.

"Hey, Alani! Hey there, Elta." Aiden lifted from his chair and moved to join them. A chorus of greetings from the others followed. Katie drew near and pulled her into a hug. "Ooh, you always smell so good, Alani." The compliment did little to calm her nerves.

Elta cleared his throat. "Look, I'm glad you're all here."

Ava flushed. She downed the wine and set the empty glass on the island countertop, frowning. "What is it, Elta?"

Alani could not look her friend in the eyes. She dropped her gaze and stared at the custom stone floor Lincoln had proudly installed when he and Ava had done the remodel.

"Alani and I have something we need to tell you."

Alani's heart began to beat so hard it took her a moment to

hear her husband's voice. She took a deep breath, trying to calm her runaway nerves. Her gaze met Ava's, and pain registered on both of their faces.

She knows, Alani thought. And she is going to hate me for this.

Her friend paled. She lifted up two open palms as if to ward off what she now knew was coming. "They don't know," she pleaded, her eyes filling with tears.

Elta placed his hand on her shoulder and took her aside. He gave her a look full of meaning. "Alani and I have learned information we must not keep secret. Please, Ava. We love you like family. Please trust me on this. You and the kids need to know what we've learned."

Alani couldn't help herself. She took her friend's hands in her own. "Tell us to go, and we will. But I agree with Elta. It is not good to keep secrets, Ava."

"For nothing is hidden that will not become evident, nor anything secret that will not be known and come to light," he said, quoting scripture. "Ava, secrets always come out…eventually."

Ava took a deep breath, nodded. "Okay. But I need to be the one to tell them."

Ava returned to her children, who were watching the scene with concern. "I need to talk with you," she said, her voice trembling.

"About the house in Hana?" Christel asked.

Ava nodded. "Yes."

She revealed how she and Alani had made a trip to Hana to see the house. "It wasn't like your father to keep something from me. There were so many questions. I had to understand," she explained. "I figured a trip might provide some answers."

"That's where you went that day?" Katie asked, her eyes wide.

Ava nodded. "Yes." Her hands shook as she told them what

they'd found—a tiny bungalow of a house tucked on a side street in Hana. The house was neat and clean. Nothing special. Inside, they discovered a woman's things, toiletries and such.

Ava's eyes filled with tears. "I wanted to protect you."

Shane ran his hands through the top of his hair. "Mom, what are you saying?"

Aiden buried his forehead in his hands. "She's saying Dad had an affair."

Katie pushed the pile of matchsticks back. "No." She shook her head. "That's not possible. Dad wouldn't do that to us."

Christel reached and covered her sister's hand with her own. Her eyes were filled with pain.

"Who?" Shane demanded, his fists tight upon the table. "Do you know who?"

Elta gently nudged his wife's shoulder. Alani couldn't help herself. Tears flowed down her cheeks as she pulled Mia's envelope from her purse. "You need to read this," she said. Her hand trembled as she handed over the sealed letter. "It's from Mia." She struggled to clear her throat of emotion so they could hear her. She looked to Elta. "The letter is from our daughter."

Ava's eyes grew wide as realization sunk in. She took a step backward, then another. "No," she said. "No."

Alani couldn't hold back the flood of tears. "She left this for you." She offered the envelope again.

Ava shook her head violently. Her eyes narrowed. "No. I don't want it. Take it and go!" She jabbed her finger in the direction of the door. "Please...please, just leave!"

Ava folded to the floor. Her sobs sounded like a wounded seal as she wrapped her arms around herself and rocked. "I can't. I can't."

Christel and Katie immediately went to their mother. They dropped to the floor by her side and comforted her. "Mom, it's okay," Christel told her. "It's going to be okay."

Aiden stood near the table, shaken. No words came from his open mouth.

Shane pounced on the letter and took it from Alani's hand. "Let me see that." He tore it open and scanned the sheet of paper. "Mia had an affair with our dad?"

Aiden pounded the table. "No. That's not possible. Dad wouldn't do that." Even as he made the claim, his eyes told another story. His shoulders sagged with the weight of the truth.

Christel leapt up, took the letter, and read it for herself. When finished, she opened her hand and let it flutter to the floor. "It's…it's true." She paused, confused. "Why are you two delivering this letter? Where is she? I want to talk to her!"

Elta explained Mia's decision to leave the island. He told them Ori had taken her to the airport and that she was gone.

Alani looked to her husband. Elta seemed to have a hard time measuring the pain in the room. He struggled to compose himself. "I know this is agonizing. It is tortuous for our family as well. We have all been betrayed by people we love dearly. This ruinous choice cost Lincoln his life. It cost our daughter her self-respect, her dignity. It cost all of us our ability to stand firm on the foundation we'd established. Our families have been robbed of something dear. Trust was stolen from us by the very ones who should have known better, done better. They made a choice—one that sliced all of our hearts wide open."

Elta was now crying. He didn't even try to hold back the emotion as he continued. "So, where do we go from here? What do we do with this pain?" He placed his arm around Katie, who stood close, so overwrought she was whimpering. "We must find a way to forgive. Forgiveness is not absolution. It does not say what they did was okay. Lincoln and Mia's actions were abhorrent. It was wrong."

Elta offered his other arm to Shane, who stood with slumped shoulders, trying to take in what he'd learned. "The only way we heal is to release them to God. Their sin is not ours to wrestle. Our job is to guard our hearts against bitterness. We do that by forgiving them."

Alani could stand it no more. She pulled away from Elta and dropped to the floor next to Ava. She gathered her best friend in her arms and whispered the *ho'oponopono* prayer. "I'm sorry. Please forgive me. I love you."

Ava buried her head against Alani's chest and openly wept. "It was Mia."

Alani pushed the damp hair off her friend's forehead. Fighting despair, she pressed the side of her face against the top of Ava's hair and rocked her. "I know. Yes, I know."

The two women held onto each other tightly, their souls knit with a sharp thread of mutual pain.

Women who shared a wound that would scar both of them forever.

26

It was nearly dawn when Ava stepped from her car and made her way to her brother's boat on the pier. Even at this early hour, she knew he would be here getting ready for the day's excursions.

Jack looked up in surprise as she approached. "Ava? What are you doing here, sis?"

She unsuccessfully tried to hide her tears. "I—I need to talk."

He took one look at her crushed face and scrambled forward, jumped from the boat onto the old wooden dock, and pulled her into his arms. "Honey, what is it?"

She relaxed against his tight squeeze, letting the strength of her brother's broad chest soothe her. "Can we go out? Just the two of us?"

He pulled back and took her by the shoulders. "Of course. Just give me a minute to make some calls."

She felt terrible watching him pull his phone out and dial. His excursions were popular and booked way in advance. Rearranging his schedule would be no small feat.

Minutes later, he was by her side. "Done." He paused,

examined her. Likely, he knew what was causing her pain would not show up in physical form. Determined to accommodate her wishes, he took her hand and led her to the raft. "I have coffee on board. Let's go."

She followed him onto the massive raft, taking care not to tangle her feet in cords or life jackets.

"Sorry," he told her. "I was just straightening up some things when you showed up."

It wasn't long, and the engine roared to life. The smell of exhaust mingled with a faint hint of plumeria, sweet and tropical. Ava found a spot near the captain's perch and sat. She held to a metal bar to steady herself as Jack turned the vessel and gunned the engine, sending them skimming over the water's surface. The engine was loud and rhythmic as the raft hit wave after incoming wave.

In the distance, the line where sky met water was turning color, a shade of mango with tinges of pink dragon fruit. The breeze was calm this early, but the wind still caught Ava's hair. She closed her eyes and focused on how the brisk air felt against her face as they raced across the water.

They'd gone about two miles out when Jack slowed and cut the engine. He drew a thermos of coffee from its spot at the captain's perch and poured them each a Styrofoam cup, filling them to the brim. He handed off one to his sister.

Ava held the drink with both hands and watched steam rise, not saying a word. She simply stared at the horizon and relished the way the gentle rocking brought peace.

"So, are you going to tell me what's wrong?" Jack stroked his grey beard. "I'm all ears."

Ava remained silent for several more seconds. She took another sip of coffee, swallowed, and tried to collect her thoughts. "Lincoln had an affair," she said.

The statement hung in the air like a coconut from a swaying palm, teetering and about to fall to the ground. "I didn't know. I didn't know a lot of things," she quietly admitted.

Her brother lowered his girth onto the bench seat next to her. "I see."

"I kept the discovery from the kids after I learned, to protect them. But they found out last night." She drew a painful breath, opened her gaping wound, and laid it bare before him. "He was sleeping with my best friend's daughter, Mia."

Not much shocked Jack Hart, but this news clearly sobered him. "How do you know?"

Ava recited the history of the events, the discovery of the house in Hana during the estate procedures, the trip and how it had confirmed her sprouting suspicions. "Lincoln was with her the night he died. She was the last one to see and talk to my husband...before he was gone." The words cut deeply, and her soul bled with the confession. She leaned against her brother's shoulder. "Trouble is? I don't know what to do with all this? How do I ever look my best friend in the face again? What do I say to my children?" She straightened and looked her brother in the eyes. "Do you know what it is like to see that kind of pain land on your kids? And, not be able to fix it?"

She shook her head. In the months since Lincoln's death, her family had become her sanctuary. Now their foundation, their entire structure had been blown to bits, like a hurricane had blown onshore full-force and destroyed everything she held dear. "I don't know what to do, Jack." The admission left her feeling even more shaken.

"Screw him!"

Ava looked over at her brother, startled. "What?"

"Screw him," Jack repeated. "Lincoln Briscoe is a loser. Anyone who would bugger a young lady who he'd watched grow up is a perv, a freak. He's not worth this pain, Ava." He paused, briefly. "Look, I'm not sure how to say this, so I'll just spit it out. I never liked the guy. He was a puffed-up show-off who made his way in life by clinging to your skirt hem. He wasn't the one who built that successful business, yet he went around bragging like he was king dog of the island. I'm not one bit surprised to learn the extent of his arrogance, his selfishness. God rest his soul, but you're good to be rid of him, Ava."

She couldn't help it. Her hand flew to her mouth, and she nearly choked. "So, you didn't like my husband?" she asked incredulously. "Why didn't you say so?"

He coughed slightly and spit into the water. "Thumper rule."

"What?"

"Thumper rule—from the Disney movie," he clarified. "If you can't say something nice—don't say anything at all."

Ava didn't know whether to laugh or cry. The idea of her giant whale of a brother sitting and watching *Bambi*, tucking away life lessons from a furry little bunny, well...it was almost more than she could take in.

She laughed.

It was the first time she'd felt even a hint of true joviality in months. While foreign, it was liberating.

A bird tucked its wings overhead and dive-bombed them as if confused by the laughter. Ava and Jack both ducked on instinct. This caused another round of laughter, and Jack joined her. The sound of their voices rippled over the water, the breeze carrying the echoes back to them. Ava swiped a tear. "*Bambi?*"

Jack shrugged. "It's my favorite," he whispered.

She nodded, letting the sun and the wind and the horizon work its magic on her. Ava drew in a deep breath, filling her lungs. She realized she had felt—for weeks—like a vise had been cinched around her midsection. Jack had effectively broken through that ever-tightening force in one short conversation. "What would I do without you?"

Jack took her hand and raised her to her feet. "Don't give Lincoln any more power over your life, Ava. His decisions don't dictate your happiness. You alone decide your future and the way you wish to feel." He gazed into her eyes. "You be the example for those kids. Christel, Katie, Aiden, and Shane... they'll all take their cues from you. Show them how to be strong in adversity, how to stare down betrayal and scoff at the pain. Steer them through these deep waters and help them come up for air."

Her brother was right. How dare Lincoln do this to her? To the kids?

Perhaps she had not been the perfect wife, but she'd done the best she knew how. As far as she'd known, there was nothing wrong with their marriage. He'd given her no indication he was unhappy or that she'd fallen short in any way.

The reality? All this pain was his fault, and his alone.

Lincoln was a narcissist. He viewed events through his eyes alone, evaluating every situation as to how it would impact him. He made decisions based on what was good for him. Yes, he'd been a good father. She was grateful for that. Until recently, she'd thought he was a good life mate. A good man.

Turned out, she'd been in the dark. He hadn't been faithful. He'd lied and hurt her. He'd paid a high price. That was on him, not her. Some things were very hard to get beyond, she thought. But anything was possible.

Last night, Elta had urged them all to forgive. Forgiveness did not excuse her husband's betrayal. Letting go meant steering her own boat. She was the captain of her emotions. No one could sink her ship if she simply said...*no*.

Ava lifted on her tiptoes and planted a kiss on her brother's scruffy cheek. "I love you, you know that?"

He grinned. "I do."

He lifted her hand and pointed to her wedding ring. "I think you know what to do."

Her gaze followed his to the diamond jewelry that had been on her hand since the night Lincoln bowed to one knee and asked her to marry him. The ring had never left her hand since that night, not even when her fingers swelled with pregnancy—four times.

She swallowed, hard.

Yes, she knew exactly what must come next. She paused for a moment, gathering strength. Then she spat on her finger and wiggled the ring until it came loose. She slipped it from her finger and took a deep breath, trying not to dwell on the white imprint the ring left behind.

"Goodbye, Lincoln," she whispered.

Ava tossed the ring into the ocean. The light of the dawning sun caught the metal and a glint shined through the water as the emblem of his love and devotion sunk lower into the sea. There were no tears...only a sense of relief.

27

Sack-n-Save Grocery had once been not much more than a small neighborhood grocery with wooden floors and a single cash register, a place where island tourists would stop on their way to the beach to pick up soda, chips, and sunscreen. There'd been a cooler right inside the door filled with ice cream novelties and bags of ice.

Not long after Katie and Jon had made Wailuku their home, the tiny retail store had been gobbled up by a major supermarket chain and now boasted a full parking lot, a bank of conveyer belts and cash registers, and an entire section devoted to organic foods.

Katie pushed her cart up the shiny tiled aisle toward the coolers at the back. Opening the glass door, she placed a gallon of two percent and a quart of almond milk in her cart, then wandered around picking up items—a box of baked crackers, some French cheese, and a bottle of kalamata olives. Jon did nearly all their cooking, but she could make a mean charcuterie board. Before moving on, she splurged and plucked a jar of expensive bacon jam from the shelf and added it to her cart before wheeling to the meat case where she carefully selected healthy cuts of grass-fed lamb, organic chicken breasts, and a package of fresh mahi.

Across the way, a father carried his young daughter in his arms. She had her thumb in her mouth and leaned against his shoulder.

Her hands tightened on the cart handle.

She wheeled past the soups, the shelves of pasta and cereal, and headed for the snack aisle. There were so many choices. Vinegar and salt potato chips. Pretzel sticks. Corn chips shaped to allow scoops of bean dip. She set her jaw and snatched one of each from the shelf and tossed the bags inside her cart. To that, she added cellophane bags of jellied fruit slices and boxes of chocolates, the kind that offered caramels and nougat squares tucked inside little paper cups. She pulled a bag of sunflower seeds from the metal bar it hung on and turned it over, wondering when they'd come out with dill-pickle-flavored seeds.

She heard a little girl giggle in the produce section as she dropped oranges into an open bag held by her father. Her mother stood close by, smiling.

With determination, Katie wheeled her cart to the cookie section and loaded up with ginger snaps, double-dip Oreos, coconut macaroons. The bottom shelf boasted a large package of chocolate chip beauties. She bent and grabbed three bags and wedged them in with the other items in her cart.

A voice came on the overhead intercom, "We have a lost little girl at the front. She says her name is Meg, and she's seven." Immediately, footsteps pounded the aisle behind her. A man frantically held up his arm. "She's mine. I'm coming."

Katie watched, mesmerized, as the two reunited. The man scooped his young daughter into his arms. "Don't ever take off like that again. You scared me, princess."

A pair of young women with tight bodies wearing beach cover-ups and flip-flops stared at her, no doubt taking in the fact she had barely combed her hair, had donned an oversized sweater that was out of place in the eighty-degree temps. Beads of sweat on her brow threatened to spill down her bare face. She rarely left the house with no makeup.

With any luck, she wouldn't be recognized as the daughter of the man who had betrayed his family. There was no reason to believe anyone knew, but it was entirely possible word might get out.

She had nothing to be ashamed of, she thought, pushing her cart faster. She was not the one who had done these horrible things.

She looked up at a sign that read Baking Items and wheeled in that direction. Into the cart went chocolate chips and coconut flakes, brown and white sugar, a large bag of flour, corn syrup and molasses, and a large tin of Crisco. For good measure, she added five bottles of sugar sprinkles, the kind used to decorate cupcakes.

With tears building, Katie turned and headed for the alcohol coolers and loaded up with wine coolers with names like *Jamaican Me Happy* and *Bahama Mama Watermelon.*

Her cart was now so full she could barely move it. She lumbered down the aisle toward check-out with the recent discovery beating inside her head.

Her dad...and Mia.

Her heart thumped painfully against her chest wall. The man she'd loved, the father she'd believed loved them—he'd deceived every one of them. And not with just anyone, he'd taken up with Mia Kané.

Katie prided herself on her strength, how she could weather nearly every stress without breaking. What was she supposed to do with that?

Her cart nearly tipped as she pushed it through the front doors and across the parking lot in the direction of her car.

"Miss? Oh, miss!" A man's deep voice from behind her called out. "Stop."

She turned to see a uniformed security guard charging toward her. His gloved hand reached for her arm. "Hold it right there, ma'am. I'm afraid shoplifting is against the law."

"Huh? What?" Katie glanced from him to her cart, dazed. Suddenly, it dawned on her that she'd left the store without paying. "Oh, my goodness! I'm so sorry. I—"

The officer flashed his badge. "I'm sorry, but I'm going to have to ask you to step back inside."

One of the store clerks met them at the front door. "Katie?" The heavily jowled woman looked between her and the officer, who had a firm grip on her elbow and was escorting her to the back office. "Jim, this is Katie Ackerman. Her family owns Pali Maui. Her husband is the chef at *No Ka'Oi*. I'm sure there's been some misunderstanding."

He straightened his black tie. "She left the store without paying." As if to make his point, he nodded at Katie's overflowing cart.

"Look, I'll vouch for her." The clerk who had come to her rescue looked to Katie. "I'm sure you meant to pay. Why don't we just check you out now," she suggested.

Katie nodded gratefully. "Yes, I intended to pay. I was...well, I was distracted." Shaken, she pulled her wallet from her bag, found her credit card, and held it midair. "I'm so sorry. I—I don't really know where my mind was."

The officer's face looked doubtful. Still, he released her arm. "Okay, then. We'll let this unfortunate incident go. This time."

Katie's phone buzzed. She pulled it from her purse and read the incoming text.

Meet me at Maluaka Beach at four. ~Mom

28

Aiden heaved the sledgehammer back and swung, letting the mallet end hit the wall with force. Upon impact, the drywall crumbled.

He swung again, putting all his muscle into the effort. Watching the hole grow bigger gave him some kind of perverse pleasure. He hadn't intended to remodel the living area. It was the one room his dad felt needed no renovation. Even so, Aiden needed a change, and that wall between the living room and dining room was out of there!

Why hadn't he done this earlier, he thought. As the question formed, so did the answer. His budget was limited. His dad had warned about going into debt.

Now that his dad was gone, wouldn't he be getting some sort of inheritance? He'd have to consult with Christel on the amount and timing. Maybe he'd just dump this old mess of a house and buy something oceanside. He'd stretch his budget and invest in a property that would require no work. Something with trendy rooms and vistas.

Debt, be damned. His dad's advice now meant nothing to him. Absolutely nothing.

He swung again—hard. After another hour of his effort to knock out the wall, his muscles screamed with pain. No doubt, he'd pay for this physical activity in the morning. He prided himself on being fit. His job required that he work to stay in shape. Still, rarely did he expend this kind of energy for such an extended time.

Aiden stepped back, surveyed his work. Maybe he'd simply hire the rest done. Yeah, he was done with spending all his time on this house. And now that Mike had hired Tiger Lady, he had more time. He had weeks of vacation on the books. Perhaps it was time to take some of it.

The idea struck him that there was no time like the present. He swiped his forearm across his sweaty brow and tossed his mallet aside. A quick text telling his boss he was taking some time off and he was good to go.

No doubt, a few weeks away from everything would do him good. He'd turn off his phone and go into hiding for a while, escape all the pressures of work and the constant needs of his family. He was tired of taking care of everyone, fixing every situation—pretending like everything was fine. Life was anything but fine.

Some things, he'd recently learned, could never be fixed.

He showered, packed a bag, and tossed it in his truck before strapping his dad's surfboard in the back. His destination was currently undecided but would no doubt include a beach somewhere along the way. Maybe he would head over to Ho'okipa. The morning surf report had issued an advisory warning of turbulent, swirling coastal conditions. Didn't matter. He was dialed in for some heavy action.

The parking lot was nearly full, but Aiden was fortunate enough to spot a car filled with people pulling out. He quickly nabbed their spot.

Aiden secured his valuables in his truck, knowing theft could be a problem. He pulled the drawstring on his board shorts tighter, and lifted his freshly waxed board from the back and carried it on his shoulder down to where the water crashed onto the sand. The distant shoreline was speckled with amped surfers paddling out to catch incoming waves. A few others were belly boarding in.

The temperature was not cold, but brisk, as he stepped into the water. He walked out several yards then let his board drop. It slapped against the surface.

Aiden positioned himself and cupped his palms, pulling in long strokes as he paddled out past a few ankle-buster waves to catch what was commonly known as the blue tube. With any luck, he'd find the perfect barrel to ride in.

He pointed the nose of his longboard out to the perfect spot ahead of where the white water was pumping. He rolled and popped up, catching the rising crest. He crouched low, feeling mist at his back until he was nearly sitting on the wave.

This was his special place—fear, joy, and adventure all rolled into one experience. Foam was our friend, as his dad used to say.

His dad—a traitor. To his mother, and to him. A man who was nothing like he'd purported himself for all those years. In swift action, he'd annihilated everything good, everything redeemable. He was a schmuck who took his pants off for the first pretty girl. And for what?

His horrible choice had robbed him of life and had killed Aiden's love for him. He had no use for liars, for cheats. Sadly, his father had been both.

The roar of the water filled his senses. Suddenly, the force of the spit threw him from his board, sending him end over end.

Wiping out was an underappreciated skill.

Back at the truck, a fellow surfer, who couldn't be much over eighteen, waved. "Gnarly board," he said, pointing. "Those Hypto Crypto long noses are the holy grail."

Aiden ran a hand through his wet hair. He held up his dad's board. "Want it?"

The young grom's eyes grew wide. "Seriously?"

"Take it. I don't have any use for it anymore." He handed the once-coveted board off to the kid and never looked back.

Just before he climbed into his truck, his phone buzzed. He cursed, wishing he'd remembered to turn it off. He could just ignore it, he told himself. Then, knowing he wouldn't be able to keep himself from checking later, he pulled the phone to his face and read the incoming text from his mom.

Meet me at Maluaka Beach at four. ~Mom

29

Shane sat dazed looking at the television with no sound. One of those home improvement shows was on, the kind where they buy a crappy house and remodel it into something out of a freaking magazine. On the table next to him were half a dozen candy bar wrappers. Nutrition was overrated, especially when you were mad as all get out.

He wasn't sure how long he'd stared at the show when someone pounded on his front door. At first, he simply ignored the sound. They'd go away if he didn't answer, he thought. But after the third set of hard bangs, followed by repeated ringing of his doorbell, he finally dragged himself from the sofa.

He trudged across the outdated orange shag carpet and pulled the door open. "For Pete's sake...What?"

Aimee brushed past him, holding two drinks from Starbucks. "Well, that's a crappy way to greet someone who just spent five bucks on a double espresso with pecan whip and drove four miles to deliver it into your ever-loving hands."

"What's in the bag?" Shane pointed to the small green and white bag in her hand.

"Egg bites. But I didn't buy them for you. They were a mistake."

"How'd you end up with them?" His fingers hungrily reached for the breakfast sack. He hadn't eaten in hours, and the smell of eggs and cheese made his mouth water.

"How'd I end up with them?" Aimee blinked innocently. "I used to date the morning shift manager." She held the sack behind her until he planted a kiss firmly on her lips. "Thanks for the fry tax," she teased, in reference to the recent urban legend about food delivery service drivers helping themselves to your fries before delivering your food.

"If you're delivering, I'm definitely ordering," he said, glad to see her, but honestly—even as hot as she was—his heart wasn't in this.

One brow rose on her perfect face as she examined him, no doubt taking in his bed hair. "What's up with you? You sick?" She looked at her watch. "Did someone forget to tell you it's nearly noon?"

Shane shrugged. "Nah, I was just chilling." He took the coffee. "Thanks."

Aimee brushed past him and moved for the sofa, where she plopped herself down. She reached and picked up a couple of items from his cluttered coffee table. "What in the sun and moon are these?"

He slipped down beside her, plucked one of the plastic toys from her fingers. "He-Man," he told her. He pointed to a blue figurine wearing a purple hood over his bare-bone skull. "And that one is Skeletor. They're from the Masters of the Universe collection."

Aimee wrinkled her nose. "Say again?"

Shane sighed. "They were my dad's. He gave them to me a long time ago. Skeletor used to scare me when I was little. He told me that was silly. He always thought I needed to man up, even when I was four."

His dad had told him a lot of things, like, "Look at your brother. Now, that boy knows how to surf." And, "Did you hear Aiden got straight A's?" And his very favorite, "Aiden is holding down a decent job. Why can't you?"

Shane groaned inside at the painful memories. Seemed he could never run fast enough, throw the ball straight enough, wax the pineapples, or plug starts in the dirt rows speedy enough. He'd learned long ago he fell short when it came to his Dad. He'd grown tired of trying.

Oh, and what about that time he overheard his mom and dad get in a big argument? They were both really angry, and his dad was yelling. "You baby that boy, Ava. He's got to grow up and you won't let him."

Well, the joke was on him. Who was the perfect one now? Certainly not the guy who single-handedly smeared his entire family in the mud. If he'd wanted to deal their mom dirty, fine. Shane thought men like that were pure jerks, yet he supposed it happened all the time. So, his dad couldn't keep his pants on. That was bad enough. But couldn't he find a stranger? Someone other than Mia Kané?

What a loser!

"What's the matter?" Aimee asked, running the tip of her finger along his ear. "Didn't you sleep well? Maybe you should go back to bed...and bring a friend with you." She set her Starbucks on the table and pulled her T-shirt over her head. She wore no bra. "Ah...c'mon. Don't be scared," she teased. "I have superpowers, but I promise they won't hurt you."

Shane glanced at what she offered, then looked away. "Nah, not right now."

Her face pulled into an instant pout. "Well, sure. I mean, I could find twenty guys on the streets of Lahaina who would run twenty miles over lava rock to spend time with me, but whatever."

Yeah, he normally was one of those guys, he thought. But

not today. Not when too many images haunted his mind... mental pictures he'd just as soon erase forever.

He turned to Aimee. "Look, I appreciate the coffee and all. I do. But I've got a lot going on right now. I just need a chance to chill."

"You're asking me to go?"

He paused, trying to think of a gentle way to tell her to get lost, at least temporarily. "I really like you and all. Can we just...reschedule?"

Aimee rolled her eyes. "I'm not an appointment book," she told him and pulled her shirt back on. Then, as if reconsidering, she leaned forward and brushed a light kiss against his cheek. "Look, I get it. Rainy days and Mondays and all that. Of course, the sun is shining outside." She shrugged. "But, whatever."

She stood. "I don't normally give guys a second chance when they brush me off." She leaned over the coffee table and straightened the plastic figurines. "But, hey...I knew when we met in the café that you might be worth some effort. So, call me."

He promised he would.

She moved for the door, and he followed. Before she took off, he ran his finger along her cheek. "Thanks for understanding. I'll call. I promise."

"That's what they all say," she teased.

He shut the door slowly and trudged back to the sofa.

What was the matter with him? It wasn't like him to turn away a good time. Especially with someone as hot as Aimee.

Shane looked around at the empty pizza boxes and beer cans. His life was a mess. And in more ways than one.

He headed for the kitchen drawer where he kept the box of garbage bags when his phone buzzed.

A text from his mom.

Meet me at Maluaka Beach at four. ~Mom

30

Christel sat on the cold tile floor wedged between the wall and the toilet. On top of the enamel seat sat a pile of romance novels. She was on her third since last night, a Robyn Carr novel set in the mountains of Colorado, after having read through the night using a flashlight...just like when she was young.

Beside her sat an ashtray filled with crushed cigarette butts. Another habit she hadn't revisited since her teen years. At first, the acrid smoke burned her throat. Several puffs later, the strange feeling came, that chemically induced rush you got from a hit of nicotine. Frankly, she might have preferred some pot, but her stash had been gone for over a decade.

When Mia found out she'd experimented with smoking weed, she'd been horrified. "Aren't you afraid you'll get addicted?" she asked, her face carved with grave concern. "I read it's really dangerous. Pot can lead to other things, stronger and more menacing things. I think you should stop now before something bad happens."

Mia had been her goody-two-shoes friend.

Christel sniffed and wiped her forearm across her nose. "So

much for dancing in glass slippers. Cinderella turned out to be no princess, after all."

She leaned her head against the stucco wall, feeling shaky inside. How could she have missed it? How could she have miscalculated and never considered that two people she adored were capable of such deception? Such treachery?

Didn't either of them care that their actions would annihilate her? Destroy her entire family? Not to mention Elta, Alani, and Ori?

This was not how the story was supposed to play out. Her dad and Mia's sordid tale was never a romance. Their choices were nothing more than a tired B-rated movie playing on a dilapidated theatre screen with rips in it. A cinematic production that flopped in the ratings with panned reviews.

It had taken everything in her not to book a flight to the mainland and find Mia, snatch the long, black hair off her head. Instead, she yanked hard on her own temper and took a deep breath. In the end, what would it matter? The witch didn't deserve the energy. Obviously, Mia Kané was no longer the girl she had loved.

Even as the thought formed, her heart ached. Yes, Mia had been her friend when they were young...perhaps her best friend. They'd built forts together behind the packing sheds. They'd taken the tops from the pineapples and wore them as hats, leaving their hair sticky. They'd played hide-n-seek in the pews of her dad's church.

As the years wore on, she and Mia had grown apart as adults, to some extent. Christel blamed their busy lives. The fact remained, there was a time they mostly saw life through each other's eyes.

Irked, she tossed the romance novel aside and dug in her purse for the bottle of nail polish she'd slipped in this morning before leaving for work. Pulling her feet from her cute espadrilles, the ones with the nautical-looking braided jute platforms she'd found at that little shop in Pa'ia, she braced her left bare foot against the toilet base and opened the tiny bottle. She loved the color—*Bee-Hind the Scenes*—a pretty pale-yellow hue. She leaned over and focused, then carefully painted her toenails. Then she did the other foot. When she was finished, she raised her legs and wedged her feet on the toilet seat next to the books to let the polish dry, wiping at tears as they made their way down her cheeks.

Christel startled at a knock on the locked door.

"Honey, are you in there?"

She squeezed her eyes closed, wrinkled her nose. It was her mother.

Silence.

"Christel? Honey?"

She groaned inside, not ready to end her private meltdown. "Yeah?" she finally said, barely above a whisper.

"Christel? Is that you?" There was a pause. "I smell smoke."

She straightened and let out a sigh. "Just a minute, Mom." She frantically glanced around hoping to spot a can of air freshener. Bingo!

She grabbed it and pulled the top off, pressed the white button and sprayed the air with some scent that smelled a lot like stale roses. "I'll—uh, be out in a sec."

Talk about déjà vu. It was as if the clock had turned back two decades and she was fourteen again.

Mom rattled the door. "Honey, are you okay?"

Christel bit her lip, stalling for time. She didn't want to add to her mother's anguish, but the truth was, she didn't want to be around anyone right now. Especially her mom. She had a bad feeling the dam was going to break, and her mom would simply spill out everywhere. Christel wasn't sure how she'd ever stop the flow.

Even as those thoughts pushed through her mind, she set

the can of air freshener down and moved for the door and unlocked it.

The door opened, and her mom peeked inside. "Christel? What are you doing?"

"Reading," Christel told her.

"In the office bathroom?"

She shrugged. "Yeah, I just wanted to—"

She didn't even get the sentence out before her mom took one look at her wrecked face and pulled her into an embrace. Christel could smell her mother's favorite soap and was immediately transported back to a time when those same arms made scuffed knees and bee stings all better. Her eyes continued to fill and spill over, and she hated herself for it.

"Oh, honey...I know." Her mother stroked her hair.

To her credit, her mother didn't tell her everything would be fine. She didn't give advice or tell her to buck up. She simply held her.

Minutes passed before Christel felt strong enough to pull away slightly. The tables were turned. It wasn't her mother who was a mess and needed comfort. Her own emotions had rippled out. "Mom, I'm all right. I just needed some time to get a grip on all this, you know?"

"Yeah, I do."

Her mother took her face in her hands and looked into her eyes. "Look, your brothers and sisters are on their way to meet us at Maluaka Beach. At four. Dry your eyes and ride with me."

Christel nodded. Through all the decades of her life, and especially when she was going through the divorce, her mother had been by her side. She would follow her anywhere. "I love you, Mom."

Her mom patted her cheek. "I love you, too."

31

Ava Briscoe arrived at Maluaka Beach and drove directly to the parking lot where she sat in the car with Christel, taking in the scenery. The view from this perch had been featured in travel magazines and websites—even wall paintings showcased in art galleries, yet nothing could capture the reality of the vista before them.

For three decades, she'd lived here. On this island, raising her children, building a stellar business. But in the last few months, everything she'd experienced had become distorted by Lincoln's infidelity.

Distorted. But that didn't mean her life ended. Her life was her children, her business, and more importantly...herself. She'd always been the cornerstone for everyone else. But it was time to be her own rock. To forge her own path. It was time to live...for Ava. In doing so, she would be an example for her precious kids.

Ava let her eyes roam across the scene outside the car window—the swaying palms, the blue water, and vast sky. The pure beauty before her. "I don't think I'll ever again take any of this for granted," she told her daughter who had her head tucked, reading a text.

Christel dropped her hands marginally and studied her mother's face. "Did you take it for granted?"

Everything, she wanted to say to her eldest child. *I took everything for granted.* Instead, she blinked and let a smile spread slowly across her face. "Humans have a way of getting so caught up in all the problems of *the now* that they forget about the possibilities of *the tomorrow*."

"You're kind of scaring me, Mom."

Ava drew in a deep breath. "Don't be. I'm good. I promise."

Christel nodded. With eyes narrowed, she inspected her mother—likely looking for cracks in her armor. After a few moments, and apparently reaching satisfaction, she went on texting with one hand as she opened the passenger door with her other.

Ava simply smiled as she climbed from the car and lifted a picnic basket from the trunk. Together, they started walking the path leading to the water. The beach was wide and long, with smooth sand and the Pacific stretching endlessly beyond. A huge cropping of black lava rocks jutted up at one end, a stark contrast against the azure-blue water and white, frothy waves crashing against the giant rocks. Even so, the water in the bay was calm...a calm that was, surprisingly, reflected inside her soul.

Since her time on the water with her brother—and Jack's immeasurable wisdom, she'd known peace. Perhaps it had been there all along but was hidden so deep in her gut that even the oceans of tears she'd shed couldn't raise it to the surface. But in a single conversation, Jack had righted her lilting ship.

Christel clicked off her phone and slipped it in her sundress pocket. "So, Katie, Aiden, and Shane are meeting us here?"

Ava nodded. "And Jon and Uncle Jack. Alani is keeping the girls."

"Alani?" Christel pulled to a stop and turned to face her. "You guys okay, then? I mean...with everything that went down."

"We can't blame the ocean if we eat a bad fish," Ava told her.

"Okaaaay."

"Christel, honey. Elta and Alani were blindsided by what happened. They're hurting, too." Ava quickly assured her daughter that her best friend remained so. She could not be blamed for Lincoln's actions. Neither should Elta and Alani be held accountable for their daughter's choices, no matter how unfortunate.

"So, then...what's up with the sudden meeting?"

Ava smiled, winked, and motioned for her to follow. "You'll see."

They were all there waiting. Katie stood ankle-deep in the surf and waved. Ava waved back.

Aiden quickly moved to join her and unloaded the basket from her hand. "So, what's all this about?" he asked.

Ava held up open palms. "Let's eat first."

With the girls' help, she spread a large blue-and-white-striped blanket out over the sand. She dropped her beach hat to the ground and proceeded to unload a full-blown picnic that included pineapples, bananas, and luscious ripe mangos, all freshly picked that morning.

"Come. Sit," she told them, motioning for them to join her on the blanket.

Everyone loaded their plates. Ava passed out drinks, then looked out over her precious clan. "I know you're all curious about why I asked you to drop everything and meet me here."

"More like insisted," Shane added, not bothering to hide his annoyance.

Ava shrugged. "Maybe, but I call mother's prerogative on this one."

Aiden grinned slightly. "All those hours of labor...yada, yada."

"That, and I had something very important I wanted to convey to you all." She let her plate rest in her lap. "About your father and what he did."

They glanced between one another before turning their full attention on her. "I thought so," Katie said, placing her own plate aside.

Shane shoved a banana in his mouth and chomped on the fruit, talking while eating. "Well, I'm tired of the whole deal." He swallowed. "I'm not kidding. I've done a lot of thinking about what Dad did, and any way you look at it, the situation is lame. I don't even want to think about it anymore."

Aiden nodded. "Yeah, the discovery sure kicked my gut. Dad's not the man I really thought he was...the guy I looked up to all my life. Frankly, I don't know what to do with that."

Ava glanced over at her brother. He gave her an encouraging nod.

"Yes, all that is true. There is no doubt I will never entirely get over what happened," she told her children.

"Nor will I," Christel said, chiming in. "There's no provision in the law that allows a person to divorce their parent. You can't legally be emancipated after you're an adult. Believe me, if the code allowed, I'd be filing papers tomorrow. I hate him."

Ava's anger flared so quickly, it took her by surprise. "Never, ever say that again." The words were level but dropped like bombs. "Your father lost his way. But before that, he was a good father. A great father. And I won't allow any of you to forget that."

Aiden scoffed. "You're seriously defending him? I can't believe you'd give him that much honor after the horrible thing he did."

"I'm not doing this for him. I'm doing this for you." She offered a pointed look to each of her children. "If you allow this bitterness to take root in your hearts, it will destroy you. Slowly, bit by minuscule bit, but believe me when I say bitterness is a poison."

"We can't help how we feel, Mom. I'm there, too," Katie said. "I'm so ashamed of what he did. I mean, what do I tell the girls? What if Willa finds out? What exactly am I going to say?"

Jon reached and covered Katie's hand with his own. Ava noticed her daughter's eyes filled, and she quickly pulled it away.

"Yes, our hearts are broken," Ava said. "In part because we loved him so. What your dad did doesn't change the fact he loved you all...very much."

"What about you, Mom?" Christel asked. "Look what he did to you. Is that love?"

"Well, that's complicated. Love comes in many shapes and forms. My relationship with your father can't be placed in a box. Despite his failings, I loved him. I choose to believe he loved me too....in some measure." She paused, gathering her words. "Despite his betrayal, your father and I had amazing years together. We built a business, had a family. We made memories. His affair with Mia can't erase any of that. I'm not going to throw out the entire life we lived because he let me down at the end."

Shane leaned forward, tossed the banana peel he was holding back into the picnic basket. "I think I understand what you're saying. Dad let us all down. But the man he was at the end wasn't the same man we grew up with."

Ava nodded, loving her youngest son for so eloquently saying in a few words exactly what she meant. "Lincoln was a man who lost his way. He lost his way, and he paid the price."

She refrained from telling her kids that in losing Lincoln—first to death and then to Mia—she'd been afraid she lost herself. A knock to the soul of that magnitude can make it difficult to walk, even to take the next step. She swallowed against the lump in her throat before continuing. "The choices Lincoln made and the decisions Mia made...well, there is nothing I can say to ever right that wrong. But what I do want to talk to you all about is not directly concerning Lincoln, or Mia...or what they did. It's about us."

She let her gaze drift to each one of them, the connections weighted with meaning. "I've spent a lot of time thinking about what this all means for our family going forward. Sometimes it's best to leave the hard things behind in order to move ahead. I want to focus on our future."

She turned to Katie. "This is what I want you to tell your daughters. Tell Willa and Noelle that the Briscoes are people of hope, and not despair. Warn your daughters that people often disappoint and fall severely short of loving us the way they should. Certainly, we don't have to pretend that bad things are virtuous. Yet in spite of that, what others mean for evil can be turned for good."

Aiden's brow furrowed. "Now you're sounding like Elta."

"Maybe," she admitted. "I've always found Elta to be a man filled with wisdom. He and Alani are struggling as well. He reminded me it takes courage—and strength—but we can take our difficulties and weave them into purpose we cannot see as yet. Someone else said the same." Ava looked fondly over at her brother. "I plan to do just that."

Shane frowned. "I'm not sure I get you. We just...walk on? Like it was no big deal?"

"No. What your father did was a very big deal," Ava assured them. "We are not unmindful of the betrayal. We cannot change the choices our loved ones made. Or the hurt their selfishness caused. But going forward, our lives can still be lived well, with courage and with joy. Our happiness does not depend on the actions of others." She paused. "Only if we let it."

Uncle Jack nodded in agreement. "Living *pono* means treating others, and especially ourselves, with respect...even when it costs us. It's an ideal that transcends humanity and extends to the entire world." He reached and tapped Shane's chest with his finger. "Happiness is not manufactured. *Hau 'oli* comes from within."

Ava leaned into her burly brother and hugged his shoulder. "For the moment, though, we are still on the road. The gap between our pain and our joy still remains. If we lean on each other and never lose heart, a time will come when our joy returns. In the end, we'll be stronger for having gone through the difficulties. If we do this together, we'll make it to our destination."

Ava turned to Christel. "Darling, girl. You have so much ahead of you. You are smart and dedicated. This is not the first storm you've faced. Old wounds teach us something...they remind us of where we've been and what we've overcome. You will weather this storm as well and come out the other side even stronger than before."

To Katie and Jon, she said, "The two of you have created your own family. Those little girls are products of your love, and the people they are becoming reflect your amazing spirit and dedication to one another. Learn from this and hold onto each other. Never let go."

Ava cupped Shane's chin. "In many ways, you are at the beginning. You have so much ahead of you, son. Your adventurous spirit will carry you far. Do not let these past months hinder you. Soar on the possibilities ahead."

Her hand covered Aiden's. "Son, you especially know you don't drown from falling in the water. You drown from staying there. Don't let this swell pull you under. Swim against the current on this one. Find a way to walk on water and find joy."

"We're going to be okay. I promise." Ava took a deep breath. "I am so very proud of you all. Proud to be your mother."

Christel wiped a tear that had escaped. "We love you, Mom."

She couldn't help it. Her eyes teared. "Despite everything, life continues to be amazing. We need to breathe in that amazing." She gazed out over the ocean at the vista with all its stunning beauty. "As long as we're living under this Maui sky, my precious ones, we have each other. We have hope."

She stood and gathered each of them in a tight hug until they were all one clump, holding each other as if their lives depended on their bond.

And it did.

Jack was correct. She had much more than she had lost. Her future was in her hands. No one else would dictate her happiness.

She'd loved Lincoln Briscoe and had raised a family with him. But he was her past...their marriage and the pain he'd caused now tucked behind a closed door. Her future did not include his betrayal.

And then, as if on some celestial cue, the sun broke full through the clouds on the horizon and something marvelous happened as the sunlight mixed with the late morning mist.

A rainbow appeared.

AFTERWORD

Well, hey everybody—Aloha!

Captain Jack here. Kellie and I are so glad you joined us for the debut story in the Maui Island Series. Don't you just love my sister and her family? I hope you'll continue to read on.

Ava sure took a hit on the chin in this first book. So did the kids. But they're strong and resilient. Each has decided not to let Lincoln's choices pull them under. Frankly, I never did like the guy. Of course, that's a whole other story I don't have time to go into. Maybe someday.

There's a lot in store for you readers in upcoming books. Take Christel for instance. She's still reeling from her divorce and has been burying herself in work. That may just change when she meets a new man who seems to be everything her ex-husband wasn't. But a surprise is on the horizon that she never expected.

Katie has a full plate. While seeking to find purpose, she battles with a new neighbor. In the aftermath of his father's betrayal, Shane makes some poor choices that land him in a heap of trouble. Aiden gets in a boat accident and a certain new hire gets under his skin while he's recovering. Ava...well, my sister is a bit lost. She puts on a good front but starts to question her life and what the future will hold. A few plot twists are in store for her as well.

There's much more but I don't want to spoil all the surprises. Besides, I have a snorkeling tour about ready to launch. These tourists keep me busy here on the beautiful island of Maui.

Anyway, Kellie is writing as fast as she can. I'm happy to report Silver Island Moon is available now, and other books in the series will be available soon. I hope you'll jump over to your favorite retailer and grab a copies for yourself. As an added incentive, Kellie has slipped a preview in this book. Keep reading for a peek at the first chapter of Silver Island Moon.

Yes! I want my copy.

Make sure you also visit Kellie's website and sign up for her newsletter so you get notices when future books in the series are available.

www.kelliecoatesgilbert.com

Well, like I said, I have a boat filled with tourists waiting for 'ole Captain Jack to take them out for a little snorkeling. But we'll see each other again soon! When you visit the island, drop by and I'll buy you a whiskey or a Mai Tai.

Mahalo!

~Captain Jack

ACKNOWLEDGMENTS

A special word of thanks to the folks at Maui Pineapple Plantation (waving to Debbie, Lacey, Mary and Ken!) These fine folks let me hang with them and see how pineapples are planted, grown and harvested.

Did you know pineapple crowns are planted in the earth by hand? The pineapples then take fourteen to fifteen months to grow. Maui is known for wild pigs and if they break through the fencing, they can eat a football field worth of produce in no time.

The Maui Pineapples are picked to order and are the sweetest treat you'll ever pop in your mouth...no, really! I had such a fun time on the tour and learned so much. You guys were so supportive of this series and my heart is filled with gratitude.

Thanks also to Elizabeth Mackey for the fabulous cover designs, to Jones House Creative for my web design, and to my editors, proofreaders and to my best-selling author friend, Heather Burch, who made this book so much better.

To all the readers who hang with me at She's Reading, you are a blast! I can't believe how much fun it is to do those live author chats and introduce you to my author buddies.

Finally, thanks to my readers. All this is for you!

~Kellie

SNEAK PREVIEW - SILVER ISLAND MOON

Chapter 1

Christel Briscoe tossed her remaining coffee into the sink and placed her favorite mug inside the dishwasher. She glanced at her watch. If she wanted to beat traffic, she'd better get moving.

After a quick shower, she pulled her blow dryer from her bathroom drawer and dried her hair. She'd always worn her hair short, but with this last cut, she'd taken the advice of her stylist and gone shorter. Trying to replicate her stylist's skills, she squeezed a dollop of product into her palm and worked it through the back and sides giving the style a chunky look.

When she'd finished, she leaned into the mirror and gazed at her reflection. She had to admit, she liked this new look. At almost thirty-five, she didn't want to be one of those women who were afraid to try new things.

Besides, change was good. She'd been in a bit of a funk. The last six months had been hard. No, not just hard. Her father's passing and the discovery of his affair with a close family friend had shaken Christel to her core, left her feeling unsteady. She was a lawyer. She liked black and white rules. Gray areas were never her comfort zone.

Unfortunately, life rarely cooperated.

Christel grabbed her bag and headed for the door, determined to shake off the past. She vowed to take the advice of her mother, a woman she admired. No one else could dictate your happiness. Your life…your choices. She was choosing to be in a good space and be happy.

As she pulled her car door open her cell buzzed. She dug inside her bag and pulled out her phone to find a meeting notification. A meeting she'd completely spaced off.

"Crud!" She tossed her bag on the passenger seat and folded into the driver's seat. She had less then fifteen minutes to drive to Pali Maui, their family's pineapple plantation. A drive that normally would take a half hour, in good traffic. She swallowed hard as she started the engine.

Christel lived in a trendy residential enclave known as Maui by the Sea. Her neighbors were mostly affluent career-driven couples with children. She was only one of a few singles which included an older widow who walked every morning.

"Hey," Maggie called out as Christel pulled from the driveway. Her neighbor wore a bright pink jogging suit with matching running shoes and waved her arms wildly.

Christel groaned and lowered her window. "Hey, Maggie. Look, I'm really running late."

"Oh, poo. Young people hurry far too much. When you get to be my age, you realize there's value in slowing down a bit. Life is too short to miss the moments."

"I—I have a meeting." Christel didn't want to be rude, but she didn't have a minute to spare. Maggie was known for grabbing more than a minute in these encounters.

"Okay, I'll let you go," she said, pushing her sunglasses up into her white hair. "First you have to promise to join me for a little dinner party. I met this really nice young man at the bank the other day. He just moved to the island and he needs to meet people."

In Maggie speak that meant her neighbor was set on connecting her single next-door neighbor with another prospect. Maggie had been trying to hook her up ever since the divorce. Like she was ready for all that again.

"That's so sweet, Maggie. I'll tell you what, let me check my calendar when I get to work and see when I might squeeze in something." She looked at her neighbor apologetically. They both knew it would be a freezing cold day in Maui before she'd agree to that dinner. Blind dates were one of those gray areas she hated. "I really have to go, Maggie." To further make her point, she waved and raised her window before backing out onto the street. Minutes later, she pulled out of the neighborhood onto the highway and gunned it.

Let's see what her new Miata could do.

Christel was barely on the outskirts of Pa'ia when she heard a siren wailing behind her. She quickly glanced in the rearview mirror to find red lights blaring on a police car as the vehicle drew near.

Her foot immediately lifted from the accelerator. An adrenaline rush kicked in as she slowed and pulled off the road. Crud! Crud!

With her heart pounding, she cut the engine and grabbed her wallet from her purse. She'd never been issued a citation. Guess there was a first time for everything.

Christel watched a police officer in full uniform exit his patrol car. He marched to her passenger door and motioned for her to lower the window.

She immediately complied. "Sorry, officer. Was I speeding?" What a stupid question. Of course, she was speeding. Her nerves were getting the best of her. She granted the officer her widest smile in hopes of gaining favor.

It was then that she recognized his face. "Web? Webley

Green?" One of her former schoolmates from high school smiled back at her.

"Hey, you remember me."

Remember him? Who could forget Webley Green? He was one of the strangest kids she'd ever known. While most of the class dressed in shorts and flip flops, Web wore an old army surplus jacket everywhere he went. And John Lennon type glasses. His hair was carrot orange and he was tall and lanky, like a new baby colt who had yet to grow into his wobbly legs.

Web had asked her to the prom and she'd declined. She'd felt bad after seeing the disappointment on his face. But go to the prom with Webley Green? Uh, no.

Christel forced a smile. "Of course, I remember you, Webley. How have you been? I heard you moved off island after school."

He puffed out his chest. "Yes, I did. Went to the University of Washington. Got a criminal justice degree. And, well, here I am...a proud member of the Pa'ia police force. I'm currently a highway patrol officer. But I've got my eyes set on becoming a detective. Per my training," he quickly added.

The sun caught his badge. The glint made her blink. "Well, that's...impressive." She didn't dare look at her watch, but there was no doubt she was going to miss her meeting.

"Thanks. I like it. What about you? What are you doing these days?"

After a quick look at the citation book in his hands, she raised her gaze level with his. "I'm a lawyer. I work for my family." She briefly updated him on her mom and siblings and on Pali Maui and how the business had grown. She skipped the part about her dad.

Web slipped the citation book into his back pocket, bent and leaned his arms on the door. Through the open window, he grinned. "Say, I was wondering...I mean, I see you aren't wearing a ring." He looked to her left hand. "And a while back,

I was browsing an online dating site. Imagine my surprise when your face showed up. Your profile said you liked a good brunch. So, I was thinking...why don't you let me take you to the Four Seasons. They have a great Sunday buffet. Unless you go to church. I mean, we could go to church together first. Whatever you want."

The color drained from Christel's face. She was going to kill her sister! She'd told her to take that profile down and never do something like that again. Why was everyone always trying to fix her up? She was just fine remaining single. Men were nothing but trouble.

"Oh, I don't think so." She scrambled to think of some excuse. "I...well, my dad passed away not so long ago and I'm still not up for any kind of socializing right now." Epic new low. Now she was using her dad as an excuse? She'd sold her soul to the devil.

Web's face filled with sympathy. He placed his hand on her arm. "I hadn't heard. That's awful. I am so sorry."

Christel attempted to manufacture sadness. "Yeah, life is short. We need to enjoy all the moments."

He nodded and slowly lifted his hand from her. "So true. Well, look...you've obviously had a lot on your mind. Let me just issue you a warning. And about that date, I absolutely understand. We can give it a few weeks."

She thanked him profusely and handed over her driver's license and car registration, purposely ignoring the last comment.

Web took her license and registration and promised to be right back. He sauntered back to his vehicle, leaned inside and grabbed the radio and spoke to someone. When he noticed her watching, he waved and gave her a reassuring nod.

When he returned, he had the warning made out. "Be careful," he cautioned, handing the slip of paper to her. "I'd hate to see you get in an accident." He passed over her driver's license and registration. "Like I said, I'll call you. Especially now that I know where you live," he added with a slight grin.

His cell phone rang and he pulled it to his ear. "Yeah, Officer Green here." He held up a finger signaling her to hold on a minute while he listened. Web nodded somberly. "Got it."

He shoved his phone into his pocket. "Look, I've got to go. There's been a boat explosion in Kahului Bay. Multiple injuries." His eyes widened and he barely bid her goodbye before he rushed for his patrol car.

Her phone buzzed on the seat next to her. Christel picked it up. It was her sister.

"Hey, Katie. Look, I thought I told you to take my profile down from that online dating site—"

"Christel," Katie interrupted. "There's been an explosion. We just got word Aiden was on a boat that blew up. He's been hurt and they're taking him to Maui Memorial. Meet us there." Katie clicked off without waiting for a response.

Christel stared at her phone for several seconds letting the news sink in. She tossed her cell back on the passenger seat. With her heart painfully thumping against her chest, she hit the ignition and punched the accelerator, barely checking for oncoming traffic before pulling back onto the highway.

Her brother was hurt.

Nothing…and she meant, *nothing*, was going to stop her from getting to him.

YES! I want this book!

Available at all retailers.

www.kelliecoatesgilbert.com

ABOUT THE AUTHOR

Kellie Coates Gilbert has won readers' hearts with her compelling and highly emotional stories about women and the relationships that define their lives. A former legal investigator, she is especially known for keeping readers turning pages and creating nuanced characters who seem real.

In addition to garnering hundreds of five-star reviews, Kellie has been described by RT Book Reviews as a "deft, crisp storyteller." Her books were featured as Barnes & Noble Top Shelf Picks and were included on Library Journal's Best Book List.

Born and raised near Sun Valley, Idaho, Kellie now lives with her husband of over thirty-five years in Dallas, where she spends most days by her pool drinking sweet tea and writing the stories of her heart.

For a complete listing of books and to connect with Kellie, visit her website:

www.kelliecoatesgilbert.com

ALSO BY KELLIE COATES GILBERT

THE PACIFIC BAY SERIES
Chances Are
Remember Us
Chasing Wind
Between Rains

THE SUN VALLEY SERIES
Sisters
Heartbeats
Changes
Promises

LOVE ON VACATION SERIES
Otherwise Engaged
All Fore Love

TEXAS GOLD SERIES
A Woman of Fortune
Where Rivers Part

Also by Kellie Coates Gilbert

A Reason to Stay
What Matters Most

STAND ALONE NOVELS
Mother of Pearl

Made in the USA
Middletown, DE
05 January 2024

47238528R00128